RETRIBUTION - BOOK THREE OF BEYOND THESE WALLS

A POST-APOCALYPTIC SURVIVAL THRILLER

MICHAEL ROBERTSON

Email: subscribers@michaelrobertson.co.uk

Edited by:

Terri King - http://terri-king.wix.com/editing
And
Pauline Nolet - http://www.paulinenolet.com

Cover Design by Dusty Crosley

Retribution - Book three of Beyond These Walls

Michael Robertson
© 2019 Michael Robertson

Retribution - Book three of Beyond These Walls is a work of fiction. The
characters, incidents, situations, and all dialogue are entirely a product of the
author's imagination, or are used fictitiously and are not in any way
representative of real people, places or things.

Any resemblance to persons living or dead is entirely coincidental.

READER GROUP

Join my reader group for all of my latest releases and special offers. You'll also receive some FREE books. You can unsubscribe at any time.

Go to www.michaelrobertson.co.uk

CHAPTER 1

As Spike stood in front of the tall wooden gates, he shook his head. "I didn't think we'd see this side of the gates again. When the coach arrives, we'll be going home. At times, I wondered if this day would ever come. So much has changed in such a short time."

Matilda nodded and exhaled hard. "I was a kid when we started our national service. I now see why so few people talk about it when they return."

Maybe Spike would get used to the feel of it, but at present, the weight of the large medal tugged on his neck. A metal disc of brushed steel, three inches in diameter and half an inch thick on a necklace of ribbon, it had no inscription or finishing, but everyone knew what it meant: one of the lucky few cadets chosen to be in the trials with the chance of being the next apprentice. It also told the guards that he still had the freedom of the city. Although, it was more for show; the guards always knew the handful of rookies due to return for the trials. It both removed the need to show them the medal and, more importantly, prevented anyone else posing as a winner to blag free movement through the districts.

While feeling the weight of his prize, the cold metal in the palm of his hand, Spike nodded. "Everything's going to be okay. One thing this experience has taught me is if I work hard enough and act with integrity, everything works out. Even if I can't always predict it will."

Matilda dragged a sharp breath through her clenched teeth and quickly adjusted her stance. Her ankle clearly still caused her pain. She smiled, but her deep brown eyes didn't. "I hope you're right."

"Are you pleased to be going home?"

A usually olive complexion, Matilda looked paler than Spike had ever seen her. It would take some time to recover from what they'd been through. She smiled. "I miss Artan. It'll be great to see him again."

"I'm going to miss you." Heat flushed Spike's cheeks.

"We have a month together. Let's make the most of that, and then it's only going to be five more months. Like you said, all you can do is put everything you have into the trials. Do that and we'll be fine."

"Yeah. I'm going to take a day or two off and then get training again."

The sound of horses' hooves and cartwheels clattered against the cobbled streets. When Spike looked up at their ride out of there, he smirked, speaking so only Matilda heard him. "Well, if it isn't the friendly neighbourhood coach driver."

"Just be nice."

"But he's a dick."

"And you're *not*. When this journey's over, you can walk away from it. He has to live with himself."

As the coach drew closer—the walls closing in on either side of it—the barrelling roll of the wooden wheels turned to thunder in the tightening space. The driver glared at them as he rode past and turned the cart around in front of the gates. He halted the carriage next to them. His skin redder than before, as if just the sight of them brought him out in hives, the driver lifted his top lip in a sneer, showing his brown teeth. "I would have bet everything I owned on you two falling on day one."

Although Spike opened his mouth to reply, Matilda reached across, grabbed his hand, and squeezed it.

The driver's eyes widened when he looked at the medal around Spike's neck. "Who'd ya steal that from?"

Maybe the driver heard her, but Matilda didn't seem to care when she said, "He's not worth it. Just ignore him."

Were it not for Matilda, he would have reacted. She had a point though: he had far more important things to deal with than the angry man.

When the driver spat on the ground, the globule landing a few feet from Matilda, Spike pulled a breath in through his nose and let it go with a hard exhale. Matilda interrupted his fury by dragging him into the coach.

The inside of the carriage could have been a million miles away from the man. Now he didn't have to look at his face, Spike could ignore him. After putting his bag next to Matilda's at their feet, he took his seat on the hard wooden bench beside her. The rich scent of wood surrounded them. He let some of the tension from his frame and reached over to hold his love's hand.

As they set off, Spike watched Matilda, who watched the national service gates until they were out of sight before she returned her attention to the inside of the carriage and said, "After everything that's happened over the last six months, it feels a bit …"

"Anticlimactic?" Spike suggested.

"Right."

The carriage picked up speed, drawing the chilly October air in through the windows. The loud rattling of their forward momentum meant Spike would have to shout to be heard, so he opted for silence. If Matilda felt anything like he did—his muscles heavy with fatigue, his heart a cold, dead weight in his chest—she needed the time to just be.

The carriage had poor suspension, every bump sending a spine-shattering shudder up through the seat. It didn't serve Spike to wonder if the driver took the path of most resistance, but that didn't prevent him from thinking it. Let him. Like Matilda had said: the man had to live with being an arsehole; Spike and Matilda could walk away from it at the end of their journey.

Matilda shifted closer on the hard bench, leaning her weight against Spike. He put an arm around her, pulling her in with a tight hug as she shook in his grip. Certain she was crying, he continued to hold her.

While watching Edin flash past outside the window, Spike thought about when they were kids. They used to spend hours in each other's company, sitting on walls and rooftops without speaking. They'd watch complete sunsets, listen to the birdsong, observe the citizens going about their day. A shared meditation, it told him what he already knew … they could—and would—grow old together.

AFTER SIX MONTHS OF NOT HEARING THE WIND CHIMES IN THE ceramics district, Spike now heard them as if for the first time. Where they'd been a background noise, a soundtrack to his childhood, their harmonies now sang like a choir, calling through the streets, easing the citizens' anxieties about the lives they lived.

They came to a stop, and from the look on Matilda's face— her eyes still glazed, her mouth hanging slightly open—she also heard the chimes anew.

"You're home," Spike said before falling silent again to listen to the orchestral tones conducted by nature. The national service area had been a place designed for function. They had no room for art. If the leaders had their way, there would have been no room for love either. But it took a lot more than utter exhaustion, a brutal regime, and repeated trauma to beat love. Maybe more hardships would come in the future, but in the time they'd been away for, Spike had found the human spirit to be indomitable. Nothing could diminish what he felt for Matilda.

A loud bang crashed against the roof of the carriage, making them both jump. The gravelled voice of the driver, phlegmy and coarse as he said, "Are you going to get out or what? This ain't a tour of the city, you know?"

Neither replied to the man, but Matilda looked at Spike through her watery gaze, her skin blotchy from crying for most of the journey. "Wanna come back to mine?"

A lump caught in his throat. After swallowing, Spike nodded. He threw the coach's door open with such force it banged against the other side of the carriage. Although the driver shouted something, he chose to ignore him, picking up both of their bags with one hand before he stepped out into the street. Like the sounds, the sight of the place reminded him of the district's vibrancy. Small mosaic tiles covered everything from walls to windowsills to plant pots. Many were colour coded—green for flowers, blue for water jugs—but some areas and objects were a technicolour explosion as if the children of the house had been tasked with the decoration.

With his free hand, Spike helped Matilda hobble out and step into the street. Either of them could have closed the carriage door, but neither of them did. Instead, they turned their backs on the driver and walked towards the alley leading into the ceramics district.

Again, Spike took in the mosaics and listened to the song of the wind chimes mixing with the tittering of children's laughter.

Edin took many things from its citizens, but at least it didn't take away their childhood.

When Matilda tried to get her bag from Spike, he moved it out of her reach. As she tried to grab it a second time, he said, "You need to rest your ankle. Let me carry it."

Despite the determined twist to her features, she let her tense shoulders settle and reached across to hold his hand instead.

A quick glance at the three guards by the entrance to ceramics, Spike spoke from the side of his mouth. "What are you doing?"

"I don't care who knows about us or what they think. You're going to be the next protector, so they'd best get used to seeing us together."

The tightening of Matilda's grip sent a surge of warmth rushing through Spike. He nodded to himself as they continued forward.

The three guards blocked the way, staring in disgust at Spike and Matilda. They looked like they wanted to say something, but Spike wore the medal around his neck. As he made eye contact with each one, he saw all three of them clock the symbol of the trials resting against his chest. They probably already knew who he was, but the medal meant they couldn't pretend not to. They wore their disdain on their sleeves, but they parted without comment and allowed the two of them into ceramics. Matilda was right: they'd best get used to seeing them as a couple.

As they closed in on Matilda's front door, Spike felt her grip tighten. "You sure you want me to come in? I don't want to get in the way of your reunion with Artan."

It looked like the words didn't come easily, the skin around Matilda's eyes tightening as she looked at her door. "I *need* you to come in. Besides, Artan has to get used to you being around too."

"And your dad? Do you think the medal will stress him out?"

"A lot of things stress him out. I can't live my life trying to appease the unappeasable."

Spike let Matilda lead the way while he fought against a rising energy that threatened to turn into panic in his tight chest. They'd been away for a long time, and it took until that moment for him to realise reintegration might not be so simple. He stepped into their front room in time to see Artan rush towards Matilda and wrap her in a tight hug. He looked taller than Spike remembered. The boys made eye contact and Artan nodded. Spike returned the gesture while putting Matilda's bag to one side in the tatty room.

When Matilda pulled away from her brother, her cheeks were sodden with tears. "I'm so glad you're okay."

Although Artan smiled, it looked to cause him discomfort.

"What's happened?" Matilda said.

Before Artan could reply, Matilda's mum entered the room. If he'd had a moment longer to think about it, Spike would have held his gasp in, but to see her—her face swollen beyond recognition, both of her eyes reduced to angry puckered slits—he couldn't contain his initial response. As a boy, he used to be petrified of wasps. One of the neighbourhood kids had been stung, and it made her face swell like a balloon. He never knew the girl's name and never thought to ask. To know it would somehow make the experience all the more real, but he'd never forget her face when she heaved her last breath. A caricature of what she'd looked like just minutes before, at least her death brought an end to the writhing panic that had taken her over. Matilda's mum looked like a living version of that girl.

The gasp still the only sound since Matilda's mum had entered, Artan finally said, "Dad lost it last night."

Although Matilda's eyes still watered, the tears now shook as if vibrating with her fury. She clenched her jaw and fists. "Where is he?"

Right on cue, Matilda's dad entered the room. His presence thickened the atmosphere as if he charged it with an electrical current. It felt like a thunderstorm waiting to break. Many things had changed in six months. Matilda's dad hadn't; he was the same short and squat man, with bushy eyebrows and a slightly canted stance on account of his bad knee.

Not Spike's place to do anything, but he couldn't fight his tightening muscles. He had to be ready should Matilda need him.

After a few seconds of the two of them staring at one another, Matilda's dad looked across at Spike, his eyes dropping and lingering on the medal around his neck. The air damn near hummed.

Spike flinched when Matilda touched his arm. "I think you should go."

A look from his love to her dad, Spike kept his glare on her dad. "Are you sure?"

"I've got this. I won't take his shit anymore."

Where Matilda's dad looked like he had a fight in him, his taut frame loosened. Deflated by his daughter's confidence, Spike saw the fire leave his eyes. The patriarchy had been dwindling for years. It had now finally been overthrown.

"I need you to trust me, Spike."

Spike finally took his eyes off her dad and looked back at Matilda. "Do you need me to hang around in the district?"

"No. We'll be fine. I'll see you later, yeah?"

It took all Spike's effort to walk away, but he needed to let her deal with it however she saw fit. The determination in her deep brown eyes showed she had this covered. She had Artan to back her up. He nodded, turned his back on Matilda and her family, and walked out her front door.

CHAPTER 2

Before Hugh entered his family home, he took the medal from around his neck. He should never have been given the damned thing. He'd won the prize for the best worst choice left in team Minotaur. It felt strange coming here after everything that had happened—especially as he hadn't called this place home for years. He filled his lungs with the fresh winter air, puffing up his chest before he opened the door.

Because Hugh had failed the test in the labs and been sent straight to national service, he hadn't seen his front room for a long time. He'd rarely come home to visit when he had the chance, choosing to spend time with his brother outside rather than be around his dad. But he had nowhere else to go for at least the next month.

The small table took centre stage in the cramped space. Tailoring dolls stood around it, watching on in silent judgement. They were appalled at Hugh's life choices. Why didn't he want to be a tailor? Did he think he was too good for it? They wore clothes at various stages of adjustment. The room smelled like dust, like an old curtain that had been left in a cupboard for years.

Although he could see his mum in the kitchen, she seemed

lost in a battle against too many pots and pans as she tried to make their dinner. It took for Hugh to close the door and clear his throat before she looked up. She froze, her brown eyes—the eyes he'd inherited—filling with tears before she rushed forwards, strands of her curly hair falling from the loose topknot she'd tied on her head.

"Hugh! My baby, you're back." Smaller than Hugh by a few inches, she wrapped him in a tight hug and squeezed as if in an attempt to drive the air from his lungs. "I didn't want to believe you were okay until I saw it myself. Oh, it's so good to see you."

As much as he appreciated the affection, Hugh didn't know how to react, tensing in her arms. He'd as good as left home at the age of fifteen. And what hadn't been trained out of him then had definitely been driven from him during national service. As much as he wanted to return his mother's warmth, his body wouldn't respond, his heart aching in the stark glare of her love.

When she pulled away and looked him up and down, confusion darkened her stare. "What's up, baby?"

While fighting against his buckling bottom lip, Hugh said, "It's been a long six months."

His mum threw another tight hug around him. "I'm glad you're home."

The best he could do at that moment, Hugh closed his eyes and drank in his mother's warmth.

"Hugh!" The shrill call of an excited eight-year-old, Hugh looked up to see his little brother, James, hurtling towards him, bracing just in time to receive the boy's body slam of affection. Where he'd been able to hold back with his mum, his little brother wouldn't allow it, forcing Hugh to pick him up and hug him.

"I thought you were going to die," James said.

"*James!*"

Hugh laughed. "It's okay, Mum." He looked at James again. "I thought I was going to die too."

James had a cropped haircut of brown hair like Hugh's. His mum did that to both of them to fight against the frequent outbreaks of lice amongst the kids in the tailoring district. They seemed to get it worse there for some reason. A smaller and slighter version of Hugh, his brother would probably be taller and straighter when he grew up. He looked like he'd have his dad's height—hopefully, he wouldn't have his dad's outlook.

While taking Hugh's bag from him and shoving him towards their dining table, Hugh's mum said, "Sit down. Your father will be home soon. I wouldn't mind betting you need a good feed."

A few weeks back, Hugh didn't feel like he'd ever smile again. Even though it was only fleeting, being around the people he loved helped light the smallest flame in his heart, and one side of his mouth lifted. He sat down at the table opposite James as they waited for dinner and for their father to return from work.

"IT'S NO GOOD," HUGH'S DAD SAID, SHAKING HIS HEAD, HIS right cheek bulging as he spoke around a mouthful of food.

Since Hugh's dad had come home from work, he'd sat at the table, started eating his food, and not said a word. He wore the scowl Hugh remembered all too well. The bitter twist of a man exhausted from doing a job he pretended to love. What other choice did he have? He wasn't a protector or a politician. The entire family had learned to let his dad get in from work and adjust to being home. Let him be the first one to talk to save the volatile outbursts he seemed so ready to deliver. Now he'd said something, fishing for a response, Hugh didn't give it to him. He'd learned a long time ago that when the man started talking, it didn't matter what anyone else had to say.

After swiping his long ginger hair behind one ear, Hugh's dad fixed him with his lazy green eyes. "You should be in the labs or tailoring with me. Why have they selected *you* to be in the trials? You'll make a fool of yourself. You'll make a fool of us."

That was what mattered more to Hugh's dad: the perception that he'd look like a fool. The truth was no one gave a shit about him, and if anyone did think him a fool, they didn't need to look to his family to find evidence to back up that opinion. Just another tailor in the tailoring district, his only bragging rights came when someone semi-important in Edin called on his services. He'd mended a blouse for the wife of a politician no one cared about. He'd loosened some trousers for an apprentice protector. All tailors were the same: they were passionate about an art that simply served a function for most. They hated how underappreciated they were, but they were just another cog in the large Edin machine.

The chink of silver against porcelain as Hugh, his mum, and James continued to eat. It felt to Hugh like he was dining with strangers. Except for the food. The familiarity of his mother's cooking always made it feel like home. When he looked across at James, he found his little brother staring back at him. His eyes were two wide orbs of innocence.

"So what was it like?"

Hugh's mum shot the boy down. "*James!*"

While finishing his mouthful of roast potato, the rich flavour something he'd most definitely missed since being on a diet of stew and rough bread, Hugh shrugged. "I *am* his brother, Mum. He can ask me anything he likes. You all can."

The moody patriarch at the head of the table sniffed, shovelled another mouthful of his dinner in, and then chewed through it while speaking. "We don't talk about national service, James. Everyone knows that."

The same shame Hugh felt thousands of times, he watched his

brother flush red and drop his focus to the table. The same shame his dad used to put on him before he chose to not let it affect him. Most kids learn their fathers are human when they step into adulthood themselves. Hugh had had his dad's number before he hit ten. A weak-minded man who, like so many in Edin, hadn't ever fully returned from national service, he belittled those he should show the most love to just to make himself feel better.

When James looked up again, Hugh met his eyes and smiled. "Ask me what you want."

"Did you meet anyone?"

"James, I said—"

"He's asking the questions of *me*, Dad, not you."

Silence fell around the table as Hugh and his dad locked stares. Although his dad's mouth hung permanently open, it fell just that little bit wider as if he might say something, but then he clearly thought better of it and returned to chewing his dinner.

In hindsight, it would have been easier to let his dad shut his brother down. Hugh now felt the attention of his entire family on him. As he thought about Elizabeth, heat rose in him, his pulse quickening. Images of her bloody face strobed through his mind, the fear in her wide eyes before the diseased got her. "I've made loads of new friends," Hugh said. "One of them, Spike—"

"*Spike?* What kind of name's that?"

Hugh ignored his father. "He made it through to the trials too. He was really kind to me on national service. He saved my life."

James frowned. "How will you compete against a friend?"

"Oh, I don't expect to win the trials."

"Then why go?" his dad said.

While maintaining eye contact with his little brother, Hugh said, "I think Spike will be the next apprentice. He deserves it, and it means he'll be able to be with the girl he loves."

"Did you fall in love?" James asked.

Time stopped and Hugh's pulse quickened. He then worked

his jaw as if practicing the words before he said them. Images of the wicked faces of Ranger and Lance flashed through his mind. They laughed at the death of his love. He smiled. "I did."

"Is she still alive?"

James' words took on a physicality, the directness nearly knocking Hugh from his chair. The glare of his parents' focus pushed in at him from either side. His throat dry, Hugh nodded. "You betcha. She flew through national service as if she'd been born to do it."

"Is she in the trials?"

"No, she never wanted to be."

"So why don't you want to win? Doesn't winning mean you'll be able to be with her?"

"We have plans to move into the labs together. She's smart, and I want to return there. It'll be a better life for us."

A shake of his head followed by a hard sniff, Hugh's dad spoke to his plate. "He's clearly too good for tailoring."

Hugh knew he was smarter than his dad from a young age, but it took his dad a while to accept the reality. It only served to increase his bitterness. Never good for the ego to be thicker than your little boy. As he'd done for the past decade whenever he'd spent time with him, Hugh ignored the man. A few seconds later, his dad's chair screeched over the hard floor as he stood up and then marched from the room. At least the drama stopped the questioning about Elizabeth. Before it could resume, Hugh diverted the conversation by turning to his mum and saying, "So, what's been going on with you?"

CHAPTER 3

Unable to focus on anything but Matilda and her dad, Spike's legs turned leaden as he walked towards his house. Where else could he go? It all felt too raw, and his family knew him too well. They'd realise something was up the second they saw him, and his mum would probe until she found out exactly what it was. If he stopped now, it would take him hours to come back, so without breaking stride, he threw the front door open and walked into his front room.

Spike's mum's shrill scream snapped his shoulders into his neck. A plate smashed from where she dropped it, adding a tighter twist to his already tense frame. He braced when she charged at him, her arms flung wide. After the six months he'd had— diseased bearing down on him on a daily basis—he had to fight against his initial defensive reaction to swing for her, planting his feet as she crashed into him.

Nearly half a foot shorter than him, Spike relaxed. After what he'd left behind at Matilda's house, he should be grateful to be returning to the family he had. He pulled her in tight. "Hello, Mum."

While pulling away from him, words fell from his mum's

mouth like she had no control over them. "Oh, dear, look at the state of this place. I didn't know what time you'd be back. I've been going out of my mind trying to keep myself busy."

As much as Spike appreciated his mum's affection, his mind wandered back to Matilda and her dad. What was happening with them right now? How would she let him know if she had a problem? It took a few seconds of silence for him to realise his mum had stopped talking. He looked at her. "Huh?"

Never one to hide her feelings, Spike's mum's eyes narrowed, and she sagged where she stood. She'd done national service. All the adults had. It changed a lot of people. Was she already seeing the manifestation of her biggest worry? Had she lost her little boy?

"I'm sorry, Mum. It's been a long six months, you know?"

Her eyes remained on him for a few more seconds before she dropped her focus to the medal lying against his chest. As if testing the weight, she lifted it. "You got through?"

Despite his worries, Spike smiled. "Yeah, I'm going back in one month."

While nodding, her voice weakened when she said, "That's great news."

The deep baritone of Spike's dad entered the room. "That *is* great news."

Spike smiled and turned to face him. "Dad! How are you?"

Unlike his mother, Spike's dad walked over to his son, lifted the medal first, and smiled at it before hugging his boy. "Well done, mate."

A flurry of motion, Spike's mum moved around the room like a spinning top. She didn't seem sure of her destination, but she needed to do something. "We have to celebrate. My boy's going for the trials. My boy might become a protector."

"Don't get ahead of yourself, Mum."

"You have a chance. How many others are in it?"

"There's six of us in total."

"Matilda?"

Even hearing her name derailed Spike, and he physically sank. If her dad did anything to her …

The motion stopped and Spike's mum cocked an eyebrow. "What's going on?"

"Look, Mum, I've had a hard six months. You know what it's like. Sorry if I'm not very excited at the moment, I have a lot to process."

"Let me make you something to eat. You must be hungry."

During national service, he'd often thought of his mum's cooking, but since leaving Matilda, Spike's appetite had vanished. A nauseating lump resided where it had once been. As much as it would have been easier to explain what had happened when he'd gotten to Matilda's house, it wasn't his story to share. Matilda needed to decide if they should know.

Before Spike could tell his mum he didn't want to eat, his dad said, "The chamber pots need emptying. You look like you could do with some fresh air."

When Spike saw his mum's bottom lip turn down, he grabbed her warm, chubby hands and rubbed his thumbs over the backs of them. "I love you, Mum. We have a month together, okay?"

She nodded and they hugged.

Spike's dad returned with the two heavy chamber pots and offered Spike the smaller of the two. Spike reached for the larger one, and for the first time ever, his dad let him take it.

AFTER SPIKE HAD EMPTIED HIS CHAMBER POT OVER THE SIDE OF the wall, he took in the view he hadn't seen in a long time. Like everything else in Edin, it looked different since he'd returned. The sun had started to set on the bright and cold October day, the red glow of it bouncing off the large lake that provided their drinking water. The distance from the gates in the bottom of the wall to the lake had seemed impossibly far. Now Spike wondered how so few made the short run for survival. The grass swayed. Maybe from ground level it stood taller than it looked, but it didn't appear to be as overgrown as the meadow he'd crossed to get to the ruined city.

Suddenly, the eviction horn sounded below. Several diseased in the field, they all perked up at the sound. The people around them who were yet to empty their chamber pots waited for the evictee to emerge, some of them shifting from side to side as if giving themselves a few more feet of space would allow them to be in the best spot for dumping their pot.

A man in his twenties burst into view, tearing through the long grass at a sprint. He looked fit and fast. Maybe he'd be one of the lucky few. Even as Spike considered it, a diseased collided with him. But the man held it off as both of them fell to the ground.

While the man wrestled the creature, one of its brethren leaped at them. The man freed a leg from his struggle and kicked it away.

Another one came at them from the other side. When the man defended against the newest arrival, the one who'd attacked him first dove in and bit him.

The man's scream echoed across the expanse of meadow before dying out as the diseased all stumbled to their feet and shuffled away.

Silence ran along the wall in both directions while everyone waited.

They didn't have to wait long. A sharp spasm snapped through the man's right leg. His jaw opened impossibly wide. The scream looked to escape his lungs as if the man played no part in the generation of the sound. His body no longer belonged to him. After he'd jumped to his feet and looked around, his raised shoulders sagged. The desire to attack would go unsated for now.

As he watched the man turn into another diseased in a meadow filled with the grotesque things, Spike wondered if the evictions were part of the problem. Surely, they added bodies to those already attacking the cadets on national service. How many rookies had been taken down by evictees while building the wall? He shook his head to himself. The numbers had to be small. Each eviction added just a drop to the ocean of horrible bastards out there, but why add to it in the first place? Compliance and show. If people witnessed the effect of the justice system, they would behave. At least, that had to be the angle they were going for. Poor Mr. P; it made it hard to trust the justice system when you personally knew an evictee who didn't deserve the brutal treatment.

Spike walked away from the wall, his dad following him. He looked at him as if he'd been watching his boy for a while, but Spike said nothing.

As happened on the way there, many eyes fell to the medal around Spike's neck while he passed them on the wooden platform. He didn't want to wear it, but they were ordered to if they went anywhere outside their homes. Some people bowed their heads while many simply stared. He did his best to ignore them all.

At the bottom of the first flight of stairs, the wooden structure creaking with the weight of people on it, Spike's dad walked a little closer to him. Spike said, "Have you seen a woman evicted since I've been away?"

"There's rarely women evicted. I haven't seen one in months. Why?"

"No reason. I'm sure I'm being paranoid."

"A little bit of paranoia can be healthy in this city."

"Not when you're relying on them to give you a crack at

being the next protector. I have to trust the system to be fair if I do my bit." He flinched when his memory of Mr. P crashed into his mind.

A man who didn't know his own strength, when Spike's dad patted him on the back, Spike stumbled forward a step. "Don't worry. You'll be fine. I have faith in you."

Spike walked down to the next level, looking out across Edin. The older he'd gotten, the smaller the place had looked. Now it seemed tiny. The walls kept everyone penned in like animals.

When they were away from the wall, Spike's dad caught up to him and walked at his side. "I've missed you a lot. I don't need you to say anything back, but I wanted to tell you how proud I am of you. How proud your mum and I are. We prayed for you every night."

"*You* prayed?"

"I had to do something with my anxiety. Hell, I would have done a jig every night if I thought it would have made a difference."

It felt strange to laugh.

"You've got your mother's grit. You won't be beaten. Do you remember when you wanted to learn to kick a ball better when you were a kid?"

Again, Spike laughed.

"You kicked that ball against the back wall of the house for hours."

"It was more like weeks."

"I worried the house might fall down if you didn't stop. There's still a mark."

"You never said anything."

"Your mother and I didn't want to get in the way. It's nice to see someone strive to be better. Most of Edin's residents let the system beat them and they make do."

"What do you know of the world outside Edin?"

They stopped walking, Spike's dad turning his way when he said, "It's filled with diseased."

"You don't question where they come from? You don't wonder if there are other places like ours?"

"I'm not sure that kind of thinking will get me anywhere."

"I went to the ruined city."

"The one miles outside Edin?"

"About a mile. And yep. Matilda got cut off from her team and was forced out there. She was the only survivor. I went after her."

"And you still got let through to the trials?"

"They said I deserved it because of that. Well, enough of the protectors said that to get me through." Just thinking about Bleach quickened his pulse. "They took a vote."

"And what was it like?"

"Another world. It was a mess. No one's lived there for a long time, but there's a lot of forgotten history. Probably a lot of things that could tell us about where we're at now."

"And was it scary?"

"As scary as hell. Filled with diseased."

From the look on his dad's face, Spike expected a berating. And maybe he had the taste of it in his mouth but thought better of it. "Matilda's lucky to have you."

"Hopefully she has me."

"You've just got to believe in the system, right?"

Spike sighed. "Right." He then pulled the skull ring from his finger and held it towards his dad.

"Give it back to me when you're a protector. Not that I think you need luck, you make your own luck in this city, but I want it to remind you how loved you are. How your mum and I are with you every step of this journey."

As much as Spike's stomach turned constant backflips, his worry for Matilda clinging onto his thoughts like a parasite, he smiled again at his dad. "Thank you. I'm lucky to have you … you and Mum."

After ruffling his hair, Spike's dad smiled. "Don't go all soft on me now." A slight sheen across his eyes caught the fading light, and his voice broke a little when he said, "Come on. Let's get back."

CHAPTER 4

The ball shot past Hugh into the goal, and all he could do was watch it. He clapped his hands, "Well done, short arse." The low winter sun dazzled him as he witnessed his little brother's victory dance. His skinny limbs pumped in all directions, each one moving as if it had no attachment to the others. The little chubby kid of a few years ago had long gone.

The elation left James a few moments later when he put his hands on his hips and tilted his head to one side. "You let that in."

While retrieving the ball and throwing it back to him, Hugh shook his head. "I didn't. It was a good shot. You're getting stronger and faster."

"It's taken me ten minutes to recover from the run over here."

"Yeah, sorry about that; I need to be fit when I go to the trials, and I want to hang out with you. It seems like a good way to combine the two. Think of it as training for when you're older."

This time, Hugh saved his brother's shot, catching the ball and rolling it back to him. Every district had been ordered to provide facilities for kids to play in. Bored children got up to no good, so they needed to do something. But with rations tight and demands on productivity high, those facilities rarely extended beyond a space for kids to hang out—usually a space that had no appeal to anyone else, so they might as well donate it. Many of the children made it their own—one person's junk and all that—and to be fair to the tailoring district, they'd even gone as far as having two goals installed to add something extra to the otherwise sparse plot.

Again, Hugh saved the shot and squinted into the sun as he rolled the ball back to his brother. They had a few tailoring work-shops around them, but he kept glancing at the taller roofs in the neighbouring woodwork district. They reminded him of what had happened to Elizabeth. What she'd felt comfortable telling Spike about but not him. Like he couldn't keep a secret.

"What was it like fighting the diseased?"

Hugh remained still, his brother's next shot bulging the net. The image of furious diseased gatecrashed his mind. Their bleeding eyes. Their snapping jaws. Friends turning. Elizabeth turning. He pressed his eyes tightly shut for a few seconds before reopening them. "It wasn't fun."

"Good chat."

"Well, what do you want me to say? You know we don't talk about national service. It's damn hard. But because you'll have to do it at some point, there's no sense in me giving you nightmares about it now."

"Do *you* have nightmares?"

Fire ran through Hugh's left shoulder when he hit the ground, diving for James' next shot as he palmed the ball away. The sharp pain helped him return to the present.

"I hear Dad shouting in the middle of the night still," James said. "Mum said it's because he never talks about what happened. That if you keep the horror in, it devours you from the inside."

"So that's what you're trying to do now? Talk to me about what happened?"

James shrugged before taking another shot.

After he'd saved it and rolled it back, Hugh said, "I'm fine. And don't worry, I won't turn into Dad."

"Why do you let him talk to you how he does?"

Hugh saved the next shot. "Just engaging with the man makes me tired; I don't care enough to challenge him."

"But he's an arsehole."

"Don't let him hear you say that. You have another ten years in his house."

"I'm not sure I can cope with him for that long."

Although he tried, Hugh had no chance of stopping the next ball. "I get that, I really do, and I think sticking up for yourself is important, but what threat is Dad? He's a dick. Hot air and nothing more. When you stop caring about his opinion, his attacks become impotent streams of nonsense."

Hugh's hands stung when he caught the next shot. James panted from the effort and glared at his brother for a few seconds before he said, "It makes me sad."

"Think about how it makes him feel."

"Huh?"

"He has to live with whatever voices he has in his head. Whatever nightmares he has at night." Elizabeth's bloody face punched through his mind, and he flinched, nearly losing his thoughts before he found them again. "The inside of his skull must be a dark and lonely space. All three of us have no respect for him, and he must know that. A lot of his aggression is about trying to regain some relevance in our family. Just keep your head down, move out after national service, and never see him again."

"Is that what you plan to do? With Elizabeth, I mean?"

Hugh didn't go for his brother's next shot.

"Hugh?"

Her bloody nose. Lance's sneering face. Ranger's fat head. "Um ... yeah."

"In the labs?"

Hugh caught the ball and rolled it back. "Right." He glanced across at the woodwork district.

A perceptive kid for an eight-year-old, James had clearly picked up on the change in atmosphere between them and said, "Learn from Dad's mistakes and don't make them yourself."

"So what, tell people how I feel about national service? Talk it out like Mum says. Tell you how hard it was and how I watched people I'd grown to care about die? Will that bring them back?" Lance, Ranger, Elizabeth. The diseased. Her turning.

"*Hugh!*"

He'd lost the conversation again. "Huh?"

"I said I think it will help."

Hugh felt the world shifting around him as if the very fibres of his reality could slip. "I'm fine, okay?"

"I'm here for you."

"They're Mum's words."

"What?"

"Did Mum put you up to this?" Before James could reply, Hugh walked away from the goal, his brother jogging past him to retrieve the ball. When the boy caught up to him again and drew a breath to speak, Hugh broke into a jog.

"*More* exercise?"

"What's wrong? You can't keep up? I thought you'd have loads of energy. You're only eight."

They left the recreation area at a slow pace, Hugh keeping it manageable for his brother.

Between gasps, James said, "So what's she like?"

"Who?"

"*Elizabeth!*"

"Oh, she's smart."

"You've already said that. What does she look like?"

They turned down the main street, the wide cobblestoned road flanked with workshops. Their windows were filled with the latest fabrics from the textiles district. Not that anyone cared outside of tailoring. They'd take whatever fabric lasted the longest, regardless of appearance. Hugh looked right at the tops of the large buildings in the woodwork district beyond. From what Spike had said about Elizabeth's stomach, it sounded like the least of what they did to her. Were they doing it to some poor kid now? "Don't you go anywhere near the woodwork district, you hear me?"

"What?" James fought for breath. "Where did that come from?"

Another sharp turn took them down an alley in the direction of their house. "Just promise me you won't."

The slam of their feet—amplified by the close walls—beat in sync. "Okay."

Hugh's chest tightened, his breathing coming more heavily. If they got his little brother …

"So?" James said. "What does she look like?"

Every time Hugh imagined Elizabeth, he saw her bleeding nose. Her scared eyes. Ranger and Lance emerging from behind the wall with her. "Beautiful. Shorter than me, mousy brown hair"—her hair stuck to her face with blood—"She's got the cutest ears. They point out slightly. Kind eyes"—glistening crimson eyes—"She's funny, charming—"

"Smart?"

Hugh laughed in spite of himself. "Sorry. But she is."

The next alley ran alongside the woodwork district. A hole had been bashed through the wall, linking the two. Most of the holes were watched by guards. It had never struck Hugh as odd when he realised this one wasn't. He'd never seen it guarded. Although, when he'd lived in the tailoring district, he'd mostly kept to himself, ignoring much of his surroundings. It made the other kids more likely to leave him alone. A group of boys hung around the gap. It looked like half of them were from the woodwork district and half of them from tailoring.

"So when will we meet her?" James said.

The naivety of youth. He didn't seem to notice the boys staring straight at them, their chests raised, their scowls fixed. Then Hugh saw him and slowed his pace, his brother slowing down beside him.

Tall and slim, the same sneer he wore for the past six months. He had a group of boys around him, all younger than him by a few years. Of course they were; the idiot clearly couldn't hold his own around people his age. "Well, well, I didn't realise *you* were from tailoring."

Hugh slowed to a walk and stared at Lance, but he didn't say anything as he fought to manage his breathing.

Addressing his gang, Lance snorted a laugh. "This is one of the luckiest bastards I've ever met." He looked at the medal around Hugh's neck. "How he got picked for the trials is beyond me."

Tension locked Hugh's jaw as he stared straight at Lance. His heart rate quickened. Images of Lance, Ranger, the diseased, Elizabeth, her bloody nose, Lance, Ranger, Magma, the diseased ... flashed through his mind, each one lasting for a second before moving on to the next. He breathed through his nose and balled his fists.

Lance laughed again. "What? You're going to swing for me, are ya?"

To see the fear in James' eyes pulled Hugh back, if only for a moment. James, blood, the diseased, Elizabeth ... While shaking his head, Hugh looked from Lance to his gang of mates, to the boys through the other side in the woodwork district. Scar tissue in the shape of a star. Angry and red. Carved into her perfect stomach. What else had they done to her? What else? He knew, of course he knew; thoughts of it plagued his waking mind.

Unable to manage what came out of his mouth, "Come on, let's go home," Hugh tugged on his brother's arm and dragged him away. James didn't need to see a fight. He didn't need to be put in danger because Hugh had history with Lance.

When they were out of earshot of the gang, James said, "What was that about?"

Hugh didn't reply. His focus ahead, he breathed in through his nose and out through his mouth.

"I'm here if you ever want to talk."

Blood, scar tissue, Lance, the diseased, Ranger, blood, Elizabeth, the diseased … Hugh locked into his rhythm and focused on his steps. Talking wouldn't bring Elizabeth back.

CHAPTER 5

S pike took the main street to get to ceramics, the wide cobblestoned road busy with traders, politicians, and children. The medal still weighed heavy around his neck as he wore it in plain sight. He'd earned his spot in the trials, he should be proud, but it felt pretentious to have it on display. The air had a nip to it from where winter drew closer, so he kept his pace brisk to stay warm against the chill.

As he got closer to Matilda's district, Spike watched the guards at the entrance. Too much going on around them to notice him, he moved towards one of the large pots on the side of the street. Because it sat just outside ceramics, they'd stamped their mark on it, covering it with hundreds of tiles of different colours. He reached down as he passed it, and snapped off a handful of flowers, putting them up his shirt before he tucked it in at the front to conceal them.

Surely just paranoia, but Spike had seen the guards beat the snot out of many a person in Edin, so as he drew closer to them, his pulse quickened and his chest tightened.

Four guards: three women and one man; two of the women were taller than Spike, and the man the shortest of the lot. His hard scowl suggested that what he lacked in height, he made up for in attitude. As Spike drew closer to them, the man pointed one of his thick sausage fingers at him. "You, boy!"

Spike froze, fighting the urge to cover his stomach with his arm.

"What are you doing, and where are you going?"

Before he replied, Spike looked at the three women. When none of them gave him an out, he held his cold medal in a pinch and lifted it to show the man. "I'm allowed to be out."

Most of the man's small and thick mass looked to be coiled rage. His hand flew to the baton at his hip, and he stepped closer. "Don't get smart with me, boy."

"I'm not trying to be smart, sir. It's just this medal means I can pass freely through the city. I'm one of the cadets due to go back for the trials next month."

"Do you want me to roll out the red carpet for you or something?"

If the man stepped any closer, he'd feel the flowers beneath Spike's shirt, but if Spike stepped back, it would be as good as admitting his guilt.

Finally, the tallest woman of the three stood aside. "Go on, son, on your way. And good luck next month; I've heard it's brutal."

Although Spike had to step around the short man to enter the street leading into the ceramics district, the man offered no extra resistance other than holding his ground.

Now free of the guards, Spike held his front to protect the flowers he'd stolen and jogged towards Matilda's house.

It hadn't even been twenty-four hours since he'd seen her last, yet Spike's pulse hammered when he knocked on Matilda's door. How would he feel when he returned from five months away at the trials?

When she opened it, Spike gasped to see the bruising on her face. From the way she leaned against the door frame, she looked to have taken more damage to her ankle too. "What's happened?"

"What do you think?"

"Are you okay?"

"Better than him. Artan backed me up. Let me get my coat."

With Matilda back inside her house, Spike pulled the stolen flowers from underneath his shirt. It didn't seem like the right occasion. And a good job too; all seven of them had broken stalks from where he'd concealed them, and over half of them had barely a petal left. He dumped them in a large pot close by. He then shook the loose petals from beneath his shirt.

When Spike looked up to see Matilda watching him, he straightened his back and let his hands fall to his sides. "How long have you been there?"

"Long enough."

Several more petals fell from him, Matilda watching them float to the ground. "You done?"

Another shake of his shirt released two more. "I think so."

Matilda set off with a limp, and Spike caught up to her, walking by her side as they moved through the mosaic-lined streets. "So what happened?" he said.

"Let's just say I'm glad I didn't know what was going on at home when we were on national service."

"That bad?"

"Worse. Dad lost his shit. He beat Mum every time they were alone."

"And Artan?"

"He can't be there all the time, but they fought a lot. Like I said, Artan got involved last night. And a good job too."

"Because of your ankle?"

"Yeah." After a pause, she said, "Something's changed in Dad. Me going on national service seems to have tipped him over the edge. You getting a medal has made him worse."

"I'll take it off when I'm around him."

"He has to deal with it. I won't take his bullshit anymore."

Because he'd been talking to Matilda, Spike hadn't given much thought to where they were walking. It took for him to see Mr. P's before he realised they'd been heading for it all along. He stopped dead.

"What are you doing?" Matilda said.

"I think we should go somewhere else."

"Don't tell me you haven't been dreaming about a meal at Mr. P's."

Spike didn't move, standing in the middle of the busy plaza in front of what used to be Mr. P's.

"Well, I'm going in," Matilda said.

As she stepped away, Spike said, "Mr. P's dead."

Matilda spun around to face him, wincing from what must have been a pain in her ankle from the sudden movement. "*What?*"

"I watched him die."

"When?"

"Six months ago. Before we went on national service."

"What are you talking about?"

"Dad and I saw him get evicted."

"When were you going to tell me about this?"

"I don't know. It didn't feel right when we were on national service. We already had so much to deal with."

The hummingbird clip holding most of her hair in place, Matilda pulled the loose strands from in front of her eyes, the start of tears building in them.

"I suppose a part of me didn't want to believe it."

"You think it was something to do with the Robert Mack act?"

"I'd guess so. That homophobic nonsense has spread through our politicians like a poison. I'm trying to keep faith in the system for when I go on the trials, but in a city where they persecute people for their sexuality, it makes me wonder whose whim the decision for the next apprenticeship rests on. They hardly seem like a rational bunch, and I am competing against Magma's son."

"But we can't worry about what might happen. Besides, Magma had your back when it came to getting you into the trials."

"You think they'll give me a fair crack at the apprenticeship?"

"I don't think anything's fair in this city, but we have to hope, right?"

A chill suddenly snapped through Spike, forcing him to look behind them.

"What?" Matilda said.

While searching the busy square, looking as far into each alley as he could see, he said, "I'm probably being paranoid because of what we're talking about, but I feel like we're being watched."

"With that huge medal around your neck, I wouldn't be surprised if we are. But if it makes you feel better, let's keep moving."

Like she'd done when they'd returned home the previous day, Matilda held Spike's hand, and they moved off, heading away from the main square into some of the quieter alleys.

In a low voice, Spike said, "Do you think someone from the government is following us? To see if we're sympathetic to Mr. P?"

Matilda didn't reply, quickening their pace as she led them through a series of tight turns. From the way she marched, Spike wondered who was the more paranoid. If she hadn't been moving with a limp, it felt like she would have taken off by now.

Left, right, and then left again, Spike looked behind, seeing a figure just too far back to make them out. "We're definitely being followed."

The next turn brought them out onto the main street, taking them back in the direction of Matilda's house. She looked at where they'd just emerged from. "I don't think today's a good day."

"We can't afford to have bad days. We only have a month."

When Matilda looked behind them again, Spike followed her line of sight. For the first time, he saw who followed them. "What's he doing?"

Her eyes on her dad about fifty feet away, Matilda said, "I told you he's lost the plot."

"Let me do something."

"Like what?"

"Talk to him. I dunno. Let him know I know."

"Like he gives a shit."

"We could tell the guards?"

"You know what this city is, right? It's a place that sacrifices kids for the sake of building a wall. Somewhere that kills you for loving the wrong person. A place where at least half the residents have been permanently damaged from their time on national service, and after they've given the best of themselves, they're then forced to live in a district they hate, doing a job they hate, most likely with a husband or wife they hate. It's the kind of place that turns a blind eye when a woman leaves her house covered in bruises. A place that ignores children who flinch every time someone moves too quickly around them." Tears now stood in Matilda's eyes, her face reddening as she looked from her dad to Spike. "It's a place that blames the woman for answering back. Like she's making the man's life harder. Like we haven't been on national service too. So tell me, Spike, what good will going to the guards do?"

After a moment's pause, Spike said, "Is Artan home?"

"It's Artan I'm worried about. He's about to lose it. He's a boy turning into a young man. There's a lot of testosterone in that growing frame. Look, Spike, I think you should go home. I need to deal with this family business, and I don't want you getting caught up in the crossfire. Will you come back tomorrow?"

The words stung. Rejection from his love and the harsh reality that the system he so desperately wanted to trust let most people down. The system that would decide if he'd be the next protector or not.

Matilda reached across and held his hands. "Everything's okay. I've been dealing with that arsehole for years."

It didn't feel okay. It felt very far from it. Still, Spike nodded.

Just before Spike set off, Matilda grabbed his arm. "Please go another way home. Don't tempt him or yourself by walking past him."

As much as Spike didn't want to give in to the man, he loved Matilda. He'd go whatever way she wanted him to. "I'll see you tomorrow."

"Okay."

"Be careful and look after yourself."

"Always."

If he'd felt anxious leaving her on the first night, her dad's bizarre behaviour had now taken it to a whole new level.

CHAPTER 6

The rain fell diagonally, flaying Hugh as if in an attempt to remove his skin. As he took the weaving path through the tight alleys, he hugged his coat to himself and tried to ignore the feeling of being watched from the shadows. He had no evidence to back up his paranoia, but he didn't need it. From what he'd learned about the place, no one passed through the woodwork district without the eyes of sentries on them, and if they chose to remain invisible, what could he do other than keep going? Where he'd walked with a hunch in the face of nature's wrath, he now drew a deep breath, lifted his chest, and focused on his destination just a few feet away.

Number eight. That was what she'd told him. The streets were so dark he didn't see the number until he stood directly in front of the door. Hugh knocked. Despite his confident stance, his legs felt his fear and they urged him to run. He remembered the game many of the neighbourhood children played. That game, however, rarely amused the ones answering the doors, and in a place like this, it would only serve to heighten what must be a daily anxiety for many residents.

Before Hugh could think on it any further, the door opened.

Any fear he'd gone to the wrong house vanished as he stared at the woman. The same mousy brown locks, the same sticking-out ears that created a silhouette no haircut could hide, the same slight frame. The younger woman she'd once been stared from her slightly wrinkled and tired face. A life in the woodwork district and a mother of three, a parenting journey that had started eighteen years ago, had clearly taken its toll.

The woman looked Hugh up and down. "Can I help you?"

"Oh, sorry." Hugh held his hand in her direction. "I'm Hugh."

The woman stared at the hand and then poked her head from her door to look out into the dark street. The night-time belonged to the gangs.

"I knew Elizabeth."

Her face changed for the briefest moment. It moved as a ripple across otherwise still water. After looking up and down the dark street again as if checking for more gang members, she stood aside. "Come in."

A slightly larger house than Hugh's on account of them having three kids—or rather, having had three kids—Hugh followed Elizabeth's mum into the front room. The family were sat around their table eating dinner. Her dad at the head of the table, her younger brother and sister opposite one another, and a chair sat beside her sister as if they were waiting for Elizabeth to come home. He'd clearly stared at it for a little bit too long, because when he looked up again, he found the entire family watching him, their mouths open as they waited for him to speak. "Um … sorry to interrupt you."

Elizabeth's dad looked at Hugh first and then his wife. Before he could say anything, Elizabeth's brother—who looked like the youngest of the two siblings—said, "Who are you?"

Impossible to hide the warble in his words, Hugh's voice shook when he said, "My name's Hugh. I'm a friend of Elizabeth's."

"*Was*," her dad said. "Or are you such a good friend that you didn't know that?"

The directness of his question took on a physicality that shoved Hugh back a step. He cleared his throat and looked into her dad's eyes. Images of his love flashed through his mind and he heard her scream. He saw her twitching as she turned. Returning to the moment, he dipped a nod of concession. "*Was*. We were on national service together." Maybe he shouldn't have said it, but in an attempt to validate him being there, he added, "I was there the day it happened."

The chink of his cutlery against his plate as he put it down, her dad shrugged. "So? What do you want?"

Elizabeth's mum straightened her posture. "Doug!"

"No, Jude, I mean it. What do you want? Have you been sent here by one of your gang leaders to claim some sort of debt she owes?"

"I'm *not* from the woodwork district."

"Then how are you here? No one walks through this place uninvited, especially not a kid at night—and a boy at that. That's as good as declaring war."

Because he hadn't wanted to appear with it on display, Hugh pulled the medal from his pocket. Elizabeth's brother and sister gasped, both of them getting to their feet to look at it, but they froze at Elizabeth's dad's instruction. "Sit down!" Even Hugh jumped.

The kids followed his orders. From the way they both looked at him—their eyes wide, their faces pale—he didn't usually speak to them in that way.

The next words to come from Elizabeth's dad had a measured calm that made Hugh squirm. "Medal or not, coming here from another district isn't a wise move. This place has no respect for Edin's laws." He sighed. "Anyway, you're here now. Why?"

"I wanted to tell you how wonderful your daughter was."

"We know that; she was *our* daughter."

"That I'm sorry for your loss."

"Why should we care if you're sorry? We don't know you, and that doesn't bring our little girl back. It doesn't mean these two won't have to go on national service in the future either." The end of his sentence faded and his eyes glazed. When he blinked, it sent tears streaming down each cheek, but he still watched Hugh, comfortable with his grief. His voice remained calm. "I think you've come here for you—and I get that, son, I really do—but you need to find a way to help yourself that doesn't involve us. Find someone to talk to. Someone that cares about you."

Although Hugh opened his mouth to reply, Elizabeth's dad cut him short. "Now I suggest you leave. If you knew Elizabeth well, then you know what this district's like—especially after dark."

Hugh gulped and nodded. "I'm sorry."

"Don't be. But please don't come back. We *can't* help you. We have enough to deal with on our own."

Ranger, Lance, the diseased, Elizabeth, blood, twisting limbs, the diseased. If Hugh said goodbye, he didn't remember it, the gentle press of Elizabeth's mum's hand on his back as she ushered him from their front room and back out into the cold, dark, and wet street.

The winter evening bit into Hugh with renewed vigour. His eyes burned with the need to cry as the icy rain threw nails against his face. His love's scream rang through his mind, and he shook his head as if he could somehow banish the sound, as if he could forget the memory. Why had he gone there? They couldn't help him deal with his loss. He had to find it in himself. They say forgiveness is the best path to healing, but scores needed to be settled. No way could he leave things as they were. Elizabeth had lived in fear in the woodwork district, and many more would feel that same daily anxiety. She'd been knocked down by Lance and Ranger and left to die. If there was a chance anyone else could go through the same thing, he had to do what he could to stand in the way of that. He had to be the justice she never received while alive.

Other than the dark silhouette of the tall warehouse between the tailoring district and woodwork, Hugh had nothing else to guide him back home. With that in his sights, he tracked a mazy path back through the tight streets.

Although he'd been allowed access on the way in, he still felt watched as he left. Elizabeth's dad was right; he'd been a fool to come here. The shadows continued to monitor him as he turned through the rat run of alleys.

The sound of shuffling feet behind him, Hugh spun around but saw only darkness. Even the shadows had shadows in this place. Where most districts had torches in the streets, in woodwork they had none. The night didn't belong to everyday folk, and the gangs liked it dark.

As the strong and bitter wind crashed into Hugh, he heard more movement down an alley on his left and then movement on a nearby roof. Suddenly, he heard a whistle and looked in the direction of the sound. No doubt whoever made that noise stared straight at him, but he still saw nothing.

The diseased, their pale skin, bleeding eyes, gnashing jaws— the images flicked through his mind.

More sounds from the darkness. They were tracking him. Whistles then ran from one rooftop to another.

When Hugh walked around the next corner, he stopped. Six or seven silhouettes up ahead, many of them holding some sort of weapon. They looked to be mostly bats and clubs. Probably all carved from wood. Then he caught the glint of a blade. Although he hadn't seen the angry scars on Elizabeth's stomach, his pulse quickened to think about them. A look back where he came from showed him more than double the number of silhouettes had gathered behind him, forcing him towards those in front.

Hugh continued forward. If he showed them his medal, they'd move aside … yeah, right.

"Who are you?" one of the silhouettes ahead of him said.

Other than it being a male voice, Hugh gleaned nothing from the dark figures. He looked at the gang. It could have been any one of them who'd spoken. "I'm a cadet on the trials. I was just cutting through here to get back to my district." Had the one who'd addressed him been one of the gang members who'd violated her?

"Then you've made a big mistake, my friend. The woodwork district isn't a shortcut."

How many of them had hurt her? Chaos rang as a shrill and diseased call through the inside of his skull. Hugh listened to it and said nothing. He continued towards the silhouettes. He saw the flash of a blade again as the moonlight caught it.

"I think we need to leave you with a small memento of your shortcut, a little reminder of who these streets belong to."

Those behind Hugh laughed as they closed in, the cackle of their sadistic mirth beating against his back in time with the hard rain.

Hugh stopped and clenched his fists. He wouldn't be forced any farther forward. Let them come to him.

CHAPTER 7

S pike found his rhythm, matching his breathing to his steps as he jogged along the main street through Edin. The medal afforded him freedom, so he might as well make the most of it. His route had taken him through the political district, leaving behind the imposing grey buildings that stood taller than many in the city. He passed the arena and listened to the excitement of the people inside, but he didn't slow down to ascertain for which protector they cheered. Then the square, last night's heads stuck on spikes in the middle of the cage. He even caught a glimpse of the bench Mr. P and his lover had sat on the night he'd seen them together.

The sun shone, but it did little to raise the temperature, the early winter air biting into Spike's throat as he inhaled. Not that it prevented him exercising. He felt fitter and more energised than he had in months. His own bed, a few good nights' rest, and his mum's cooking all helped.

The people of Edin watched Spike pass by, his heavy medal slapping against his chest with his bouncing run.

The same guards often stood between the same areas, so when Spike ran towards ceramics, the three women and the short man were there like always. The women all smiled at him, and the man glared.

Large clouds of condensation billowed in front of Spike with his hard exhales. The slap of his feet bounced off the single-storey walls on either side of the narrow road. Just over three weeks left until the trials, and he'd make sure he went into them as fit as he'd ever been. He had to win every task. There could be no room for judgement on who should be the next apprentice.

Where Spike expected to be welcomed into ceramics to the sound of wind chimes, his blood turned cold when he heard something very different. A woman screamed, her voice unrestrained with panic. "It was self-defence! It was self-defence!"

Spike quickened his pace, and when he rounded the next corner, he found a crowd outside Matilda's house. He didn't want to believe she was the screaming woman, but he couldn't avoid the red-faced and tear-streaked reality. A bear of a guard standing at least six feet and four inches tall had a hold of her while she did her best to twist free from his grip. She screamed again, "It was self-defence!"

Another guard blocked Spike's way, but he had a greater will than her and pushed through. On any other day, she might have drawn her baton; who knew why she chose to let him pass today. What looked like most of Matilda's neighbours had crowded around her and her house. The congestion of bodies prevented him from getting to her, so he went to the house and peered in.

Despite everything Spike had seen on national service, nothing prepared him for that moment. Were he not close to a neighbouring building, his legs would have failed him. While leaning against the brightly coloured wall for support, he continued to stare through the open door. Every inch of Matilda's front room glistened with spilled blood. Both Matilda's mum and dad lay on their backs dead. Her mum's head was misshapen across the brow from where she'd clearly been bludgeoned to death. The handle of a knife protruded from her dad's right eye as if it had been used to pin him to the floor.

Four guards emerged from the house, a writhing Artan in their grip. It took the strength of all four to contain him, all of them as caked in blood as the front room. The whites of Artan's eyes and teeth stood out from his crimson mask.

All the while, Matilda continued to scream the same words as if her shock had trapped her brain in a loop. "It was self-defence!"

It hurt Spike's heart to see her in such a state. A dense press of bodies still between them, he shoved his way over, ignoring the tuts and snark thrown at him.

The guard holding Matilda locked on Spike as he approached.

Spike raised his hands and fought to keep the wobble from his voice, adrenaline surging through him. "What's she done?"

A tight twist cramped the guard's thick features as if he might swing for him, but when Spike offered no counter to his aggression, the guard relaxed his wide frame. "Nothing, we just need to keep her away. It's the boy we want."

Despite standing no more than a few feet from him, Matilda didn't seem to have noticed Spike. "Tilly!"

Locked in her battle with the guard, she shouted again, "You *can't* take him away."

The guard clenched his square jaw as he wrestled with her.

Spike stepped closer, and the guard's broad frame tensed again, but he focused on Matilda rather than her captor. "Tilly! Please calm down. This isn't getting you anywhere." Although he waited for her response, none came.

The guard said, "You need to step back now. I can't deal with both of you. Don't make me draw my baton."

Spike ignored him; he needed to get Matilda away from there. "*Matilda!* Listen to me. You're going to end up in prison too."

"*Sir!*" the guard said. "I have the power to take that medal from around your neck. Don't make me ask you again. *Step back*."

Spike stepped forward. "Matilda." This time they made eye contact. She looked like a spooked animal who'd just staggered from a bush fire. Her eyes rolled in her head, and her chest rose and fell rapidly. Although she focused on him, she only managed to hold it for a second before her eyes rolled again.

"*Sir!*" the guard said again.

"Give her to me."

"I can't do that."

"Are you arresting her?"

"No. The boy did it."

Matilda turned on the guard, spraying his face with spittle as she said, "The boy didn't do anything. It was self-defence!"

A fraction of a second later, the guard had his baton raised above his head. His features turned dark with his intention, his muscly shoulders powerful enough to hammer her into the ground like a wooden peg. Spike stepped between them, lifting his arm to block the man's blow as he eased Matilda away.

Although he panted, his knuckles white around his baton's handle, the guard didn't bring it down on them. He clenched his teeth. "You need to hand her back over."

"How about I take her away from here? We'll come back later and clean up. You said yourself that she's not the one being arrested."

"That was before she spat at me."

"She didn't do that on purpose. Please have some compassion for her situation. That's her *entire* family in that house."

The guard relaxed a little, appraising Spike for a few seconds. He lowered his baton. "Don't make me regret this, boy."

"I won't, sir. Thank you." Spike used all his strength to drag Matilda away while the crowd watched on. It took for him to feel the dampness of her clothes to realise she also wore the spilled blood of her parents.

WHEN THEY WERE AWAY FROM MATILDA'S HOUSE AND IN THE square in front of what had once been Mr. P's, Matilda looked at Spike, and for the first time, he saw the girl he recognised in her eyes. "Oh, Spike. What a mess."

They were sat on the wall of a small decorative pool of water, the bottom filled with wishing stones thrown in by the local kids. "What happened?"

First, her bottom lip buckled, and then Matilda cried, sobbing so hard she wailed as if something inside her had ripped.

For the next few minutes, Spike held onto his love, rocking her gently while trying to ignore the feeling of her blood-soaked clothes.

"Artan and I went out because he was nowhere to be seen."

"Your dad?"

She nodded. "We wouldn't have left her on her own if we'd have known he was coming back. The blood, Spike, it covered the *entire* room."

"I saw it."

"We were only gone for a few minutes. We wanted to get some more rations. We wouldn't have left her if we'd have known."

"So you came back and found your mum like that?"

"He'd picked up a rock from the garden and caved her skull in. He still had it in his hand when he charged at Artan. Before I knew it, Artan had picked up a knife and stabbed him."

The image of Matilda's mum and dad in the front room flashed through Spike's mind. An image it would take him a lifetime to forget.

"Mum must have screamed when he attacked her, because by the time he and Artan started fighting, the neighbours had gathered outside."

"Which is why they only took Artan away? I'm sorry to drag you from there, but I could only see things getting worse between you and the guard."

When Matilda looked at him, her brown eyes shifted from one of his to the other as if searching his face would reveal an answer. "What are we going to do?"

What could he tell her? To trust the system? That they'd recognise Artan's innocence and set him free? They lived in a city where you got evicted for being gay. "I think we need to take it one step at a time. We need to clean your house first. I'll do the worst parts so you don't have to look at them. Then we'll have to find a way to get to Artan."

Even as Spike said it, the truth of her situation screamed at him, daring him to speak it. Artan had killed someone. They were screwed.

CHAPTER 8

"Where are you going at this time, boy?"

Instead of answering his dad, Hugh kept his head down to hide his face as he shoulder barged him out of the way. A loud bang resulted from the man falling against a cupboard in their front room.

"Oh, shit, you didn't just do that."

Although he had an awareness of his dad limbering up as if to fight, Hugh kept his attention on the floor. He might have adopted the pose of a pugilist, but the man had nothing but hot air running through his decrepit frame, his fingers twisted and gnarled from a lifetime of pinching needles.

The sound of his dad's heavy breaths behind him, Hugh stepped out of the house into the early October morning. A layer of frost ran a white fuzz over his surroundings. In the next few hours, many of the district's tailors would be heading to work. It was why he left so early. He needed to be alone.

Although not heavy, the straps of Hugh's backpack restricted his shoulders when he broke into a jog, his breath billowing out in front of him as he found his rhythm. The cold wormed into his joints, leaving his knuckles sore. At least he had a scarf on; it would do something against the frigid bite of the early morning air.

In the several years Hugh had been away from the tailoring district, not much had changed. Yet, as he looked at it through his older eyes, everything had. The uniformity of the shops made it hard for their posh and privileged visitors to choose one from another. It had been done by design to create a level playing field amongst the tailors. Although, truth be told, they'd do a similar job whoever you visited. Not that he'd say that to one of the many *distinguished* masters of cloth, their egos demanding they get recognised as the best in their generation.

As he found his rhythm, Hugh let some of the tension from his frame. He rounded a right-angled bend and came across a child no older than James in the street. When the boy saw Hugh's face, he gasped, broke into tears, and ran to the other side of the road.

Although he watched the kid, Hugh continued at the same pace, every step against the hard ground sending a snapping jolt up through his body. It disturbed the swelling on his face, each stomp sending a streak of electricity through his tender and swollen skin.

Passing the recreation ground, Hugh looked at the goal he'd played in with James a few days previously. Even smiling hurt. The boy would be fine when he left. Hell, he'd probably be better for it. Hugh could see how his presence unsettled the kid. It wasn't like he could teach him anything because when James went on national service, he'd be going with his mum's philosophy rather than his dad's. A pragmatist who saw the importance of talking and knew how to express himself, hopefully that would get him through.

On his way out of the tailoring district, the medal heavy

around his neck, Hugh made eye contact with the one guard standing there. The woman flinched to look at him, but when he held up his medal, she dipped her head and stood aside.

Despite the early hour, there were plenty of people on Edin's main street. Carts carried supplies. Guards moved from their home district to the one they policed. There were teenagers who looked like they were in training, preparing for their time on national service. Of all the people, the teenagers stared at Hugh's medal the most. He ignored them. If only they knew what lay ahead.

The busier environment encouraged Hugh to pull his scarf up to cover the lower half of his face, leaving just his eyes and above visible. White clouds of condensation pushed out through the fabric. It also took the bite from the air he breathed.

The textiles district sat next to tailoring, so after a minute or two, Hugh made his medal visible again and headed towards the guard checking who went in and out. He expected he'd have to reveal his face but hoped they wouldn't search his bag.

If the guard cared, he didn't show it, letting Hugh through with barely a glance in his direction. In a place like Edin, disobeying the rules came with a heavy punishment. Many of the guards had grown complacent, putting far too much trust in the state-sponsored deterrent that was eviction.

Olga had helped Hugh in many ways, his fitness above all. When he'd first started training with her, he'd vomit after about fifteen minutes. By the time he'd left national service, he felt like he could run forever. Her training, coupled with the loss of Elizabeth, had taught him to switch off. To ignore what his brain told him about his limits.

The textiles district had a central plaza, where they hung a lot of their fabrics to dry. When Hugh jogged into it, he found it empty, as he'd hoped it would be. A large pool filled with the water used for washing their materials and surrounded by a red brick wall sat in the centre of the space.

All the buildings overlooking the plaza were used for industry and, being too early for anyone to have started work yet, currently sat empty as well. As Hugh sat on the red brick wall, he checked for people again before slipping his bag from his shoulders and unbuttoning it. He had last night's top inside. Covered in blood, he'd wrapped it around the knife. Just as he reached in to remove it, the sounds of footsteps approached.

Hugh's pulse raced from zero to overdrive. Fight or flight. The steps entered the plaza. A girl appeared, no older than twelve. She stared at him and froze.

The scarf hid so much of Hugh's face the girl had no way of recognising him. She opened her mouth as if about to speak, but before she could, Hugh growled at her.

The girl hugged herself as if the temperature had suddenly dropped.

He then hissed.

The girl turned and ran, leaving the square empty again, her footsteps growing fainter until they vanished.

Hugh quickly removed his bloody top and dropped it into the pool. The blood turned the water around it pink. He then dropped the knife in after it, glanced around one last time, stood up, and ran back the way he'd come from.

NOW BACK IN THE TAILORING DISTRICT, HUGH PLANNED TO GO straight home. His old man would have left the house by now, and he needed the rest. But as he approached the gap in the wall between tailoring and woodwork, a boy stepped through.

The tall frame of Lance Cull appeared. A grease stain of a person, he blocked Hugh's way, his hands on his hips—not that it would take much to knock him down. His usual smile, he said, "If it's not our district's hero."

Hugh kept his attention on the ground, his face still covered by his scarf. Just a few feet separated them.

"What's wrong, boy? Too afraid to look at me?"

Again, Hugh didn't reply. Elizabeth and her bleeding nose smashed into his memory. Lance and Ranger laughing. The star on her stomach. The knife going in, blood belching from the deep wound. Dark red blood.

"I don't know why you're doing all this training anyway. Seems like a waste of time, if you ask me. I mean, look at you. You're hardly built to win the trials. You might as well give up now."

His focus still on the ground, Hugh watched his breaths. Elizabeth, blood, Ranger, Lance. A deep gash in a firm stomach. The knife so sharp it was like cutting into wet mud. He had Lance on his own. That might not happen again.

"So," Lance continued, "I've just come back from the woodwork district. They tell me they want some fresh meat for the gangs. Asked if I knew any boys. They like them young. They like to break them in early. Get them subservient to the cause. You know anyone like that?"

This time, Hugh looked up, stinging lightning bolts streaking away from his narrowing eyes.

"There he is. It ain't that cold, you know. Why are you so covered up?"

Elizabeth, Ranger, blood. A diseased's shrill scream ran through Hugh, making him flinch. Lance's sneering face, the same sneer he wore in national service. Then Hugh pulled down the scarf and threw his hood back.

Lance's mouth fell open, his lazy eyes widening. The tall and skinny boy's bottom jaw worked, but he spoke no words.

While staring at him, Hugh watched Lance step back through

the gap he'd just entered through until he vanished from sight. The sound of his feet took off as he sprinted away.

Hugh waited for a few seconds and stared at the gap. When nothing else happened, he pulled his hood over his head, dragged his scarf up to cover his mouth, and broke into a jog back in the direction of his house.

CHAPTER 9

Training, training, training. Whatever tasks he had, Spike used them as an excuse to train harder. Sweat ran into his eyes as he ran in the direction of the justice department's building, his pace quickening on account of his unease at being inside the political district. The place spoke of authority. Of the establishment. Of condemnation. A district designed by politicians, for politicians. This was their world and you knew it.

The grey buildings stood at least one storey taller than most of the others in Edin. The stone structures loomed over Spike. The design almost gave them a voice as if they were the front line in questioning his decision to visit in the first place. He reached up for the medal around his neck, the cold metal disc offering little reassurance, but he had every right to be here. As long as he had his symbol of the trials with him, he could go wherever he liked … within reason.

The large foyer in the justice department's building amplified the sounds of Spike's heavy breaths. He should have gathered himself before entering. *Too late now*. He walked towards the desk slowly to help him recover, his steps beating an echoing metronome in the cavernous space.

A door flew open on Spike's right as if driven wide by the guffawing of the three men who emerged from it. To see the politicians stopped him dead. They also halted. He only recognised one of them, notorious as a hero or a villain, depending on how you viewed him: Robert Mack.

A wiry man, his face glistening with what looked like grease, he raised a cautious smile in Spike's direction. It revealed two overdeveloped and yellowed incisors as if the savagery of human ancestry had made one last bid for survival in him. When his eyes fell to the medal around Spike's neck, he laughed. "Well, well, look at what we have here; someone due for the trials." He addressed the men with him. "Gents, do you mind if I bend the ear of this fine citizen? The young wannabes often remind me what it is to be alive. They're so full of spunk."

From the way they regarded Spike, they wanted to question Robert Mack's decision. From the way they deferred to him, they clearly didn't have the authority. A subservient shrug from each, they walked back through the door they'd exited through.

Sporting a grin almost as wide as his head, Robert Mack moved closer.

With just a few feet between them, Spike's fight or flight kicked in, and it took all he had to refrain from balling his fists. The thud of his pulse a tribal beat in his skull, if he could have ended the man right there and gotten away with it, he would have. The breathing he'd fought to manage ran away with him again in the face of the man responsible for the eviction of so many people because he didn't agree with how they chose to live their lives— the man responsible for evicting Mr. P and his lover.

"What's your name, boy?"

It took a second to get the words past his dry throat. "William, sir."

A nod as if he approved, Robert Mack came close enough to put an arm around Spike's shoulder. As he breathed—half in through his nose, half through his mouth—he snorted. "Now understand this, boy. I ain't a fag."

Fire lifted beneath Spike's cheeks. "I never said you were, sir."

"I mean, can't a man put an arm around another man without wanting to be intimate with him?"

Spike chose not to answer, a slow writhe turning through him at the man's close proximity. He had to remember why he'd come here: Artan needed him. Whatever else happened, Artan needed him.

"How long 'til the trials, boy?"

"Just under three weeks, sir."

"You ready?"

"I'm training every day."

Robert Mack pulled Spike in even closer. The truffling snort sounded like he thirsted for Spike's scent, but he could have simply been breathing. A slight glaze ran across his eyes and he licked his lips. He then shook his head as if to help him break from his own trance. "Very good. So what do you think of fags, boy?"

A thousand curses screamed through Spike's mind so loud they damn near made his ears ring, but he had to think of Artan. If he had any chance of seeing him today, he had to keep the peace. The words almost didn't come, the thoughts of Mr. P and his lover being killed in front of him. "I *hate* them, sir. I think they should all be evicted from Edin. Now I'm not homophobic," he said—the utterance of every bigot he'd ever met—"but I feel like they're a waste of the city's resources. We need to work towards growth, both with increasing Edin's footprint *and* population. What good is one without the other?"

With every point Spike made, Robert Mack's smile spread until his large incisors were on full display and glistening as if the thought of evicting homosexuals made him ravenous.

"So what are you here for today?"

It took a moment for Spike to temper the utter disdain he had for the man. "There's been a terrible mix-up. A very good friend of mine has been imprisoned, so I've come to see him. I came last week, and they told me visiting was today."

"So here you are."

"Here I am."

As Robert Mack pulled away, Spike fought against his desire to look for a grease stain where the hot, sweaty man had been pressed against him. "Well, good luck, son. I hope you manage to get everything sorted with your friend. Our justice system is a fair one—we pride ourselves on that—so I'm sure everything will be fine." A lie delivered with utter certainty. From the look on the man's face, Spike wondered if his life as a politician had removed his ability to discern fact from fiction.

The wiry snake then drove a hard slap against Spike's back, sending him stumbling forward a couple of steps and leaving a stinging patch between his shoulder blades.

Robert Mack walked away. What Spike would give to be able to cave his head in …

It took for Spike to look at the woman in reception to realise she'd been watching him. How much of the interaction had she heard? What thoughts did she have on gay people? By agreeing with Robert Mack, had he just screwed over his chances of seeing Artan? Only one way to find out.

When he got to the desk, Spike cleared his throat. "Um, hi."

The receptionist looked at him, her slack face leaving white bands along the bottom of each eye. A slim woman in her twenties, she had dark skin, not as dark as Spike's, but not as light as Matilda's. Her mouth hung agape at the presence of the horrible boy in front of her. Black hair scraped back in a ponytail, dead straight strands left to hang down either side of her face gave an ominous frame to her displeasure.

"I'm not a homophobe," Spike said.

"You sounded like one to me."

"What else was I supposed to say? We all know what kind of rules Robert Mack makes. I want to cause as few waves as possible."

"So you gave up your morals like a puppy wanting its belly tickled?" The woman sighed. "What do you want?"

"I came here last week to see someone who's been wrongly imprisoned. I—"

"Did I ask for your life story?"

"I've come to see Artan Sykes."

"He's not allowed any visitors."

"But I was told last week to come back today. That today's the day for visiting."

"It is. Just not for him. After what he did to his dad, we've decided to keep him in solitary for the next few years. And then, when he's of age, we're going to send him out into the wild as a lesson to everyone else. It's a shame we can't send him now, but we don't want a riot on our hands. We can't evict minors."

Every sentence drove a harder gut punch into Spike. What would he tell Matilda? "There must be something I can do."

"There is."

"What?"

"Go home."

"No." How could he go back to Matilda?

"No? You like that medal around your neck?"

Spike chose not to reply.

"We have the power to take it away. Now go home and give up on the murdering little shit."

"It was self-defence."

"Said every murderer ever. Other than his sister, no one else has backed up that statement."

"I'm backing it up."

"And you were there?"

The tension winding tighter, if Spike remained, he'd just make things worse. He had nearly three weeks until the trials. They could think of some other way to see Artan in that time. He turned his back on the woman without another word and walked out of there. He needed to return to Matilda so they could work out a new plan.

NEARLY A WEEK HAD PASSED SINCE ARTAN HAD KILLED HIS DAD, and Matilda hadn't stopped crying in that time. As she sat in her front room, the place now clear of blood—it took several days to clean it, and for the next few after that Spike kept finding small stains they'd missed the first time around—she held her head in her hands. "So unless we have a witness that says what happened, they're going to treat Artan like he's a murderer?"

"That's pretty much what she said."

"But the neighbours won't even talk to me, let alone give a statement. They saw Mum as either weak for taking a beating, or moaning for complaining about it. No one ever judged that arse-hole of a man despite how violent he got. Even the guards turned a blind eye. What's wrong with this city? Men are allowed to break because of their experience on national service, even if women and children are the victims. All the while, the rest of us have to hold it together and keep our mouths shut. As long as they get their precious, bloody wall extended, who gives a shit, right? And the neighbours are even less likely to help now you've moved in—"

"Would it help for me to move out?"

"*No.*" When she lifted her face, her cheeks blotchy with her grief, the fire that had driven her words left her. "Unless you *want* to move out? I can imagine it's draining being here, and you need to be ready to compete next month."

"I'd hate to move out. I want to do everything I can to help."

"I'm out of ideas, Spike. It's not like we're going to get any neighbours to come forward, and who else will help us? If the receptionist gave you a hard time, what will the politicians do if you try to talk to them about it?"

The thought of Robert Mack made Spike shudder. And then it hit him. "Bleach."

"Bleach?"

"I could go and see him. See if he can help."

"But you two hardly parted on good terms. He voted *against* you for the trials."

"So he *owes* me."

"He won't see it like that."

"You have anything better?"

Another wave of tears derailed Matilda. Spike waited for her to compose herself. "I suppose it's not going to do any harm."

"No. I'll go and see him in the morning. It's something. We have to hold onto hope until there is none. And as long as Artan's alive, there's hope."

"I wish I had the faith in the system that you do."

"I don't have a choice. Our destiny and happiness relies on faith in the system."

Matilda's eyes filled again and she said, "God help us."

CHAPTER 10

"Hey," Hugh said as he walked into the front room, a box in his hands. "Look what I found under my bed."

On account of it being a Saturday morning and James being eight years old, he had to find things to keep himself busy lest he drive everyone in the house crazy. At present, he sat at the table, hunched over a piece of paper with a stick of charcoal in his small grip. He nodded at the box. "What's in there?"

"Clear a space." After putting the box on the table, Hugh pulled out some crudely carved models. "I made these when I was your age. Look …" He pulled out a taller and wider section that had a thicker base than it did top. It stood about twelve inches tall and stretched about twenty inches wide. The models were only six inches at the most. "It's a wall."

To be fair to James, he needed the guided tour to make sense of Hugh's creations. While pointing at the smaller models, James said, "And these are the protectors?"

"Right!"

James shoved his drawing aside and pulled some of the figures from the box, helping Hugh set up the models. When he pulled one out that had a missing arm, he showed it to his brother. "And what's this?"

"Well, it might have once been an attempt at Crush."

"With only one arm?"

"*Attempt.* Whenever I failed with a model, they earned their space on the other side of the wall."

While smiling to himself, James put the poorly carved figurine outside Edin's perimeter. "I hope I get through to the trials like you."

Ranger, Lance, Elizabeth, the deep cut, dark blood, the diseased …

"Hugh?"

A shake of his head to help him return to the moment, Hugh said, "Sorry." He removed his medal from his inside pocket and hung it around his brother's neck.

James straightened his back and beamed a grin. "What was it like?"

When Hugh opened his mouth, James cut him off. "And spare me the bullshit. I'm old enough to hear it."

Snapping mouths. Yellow teeth. Spasming limbs. The images crashed into Hugh's mind like meteors dashing a planet.

"You know how important it is to talk about it, right?"

"You've been spending too much time with Mum."

"You think I stand a better chance by learning from Dad?"

What could he tell his brother of his experience? The pain in his heart had no words. The limitations of the human language had no chance approximating what he'd been through. Besides, what good would it do? It would change nothing and help no one, but his brother needed something; otherwise, he'd keep asking. "I met all the protectors."

"*All* of them?"

"Yep."

"Even *Magma*?"

"You should be asking about Warrior. Sure, Magma's a leader. Stoic, strong, powerful. But Warrior? He's insane."

"And that's a good thing?"

"You have to be nuts to be a protector. Also, I looked after the weapons for my team. They came apart easily, so I made sure they were maintained. You need to make sure you do the same. It would be a shame for you or your team to die from such a preventable cause." Thoughts of Olga and Max. Of Ranger's smug grin. Elizabeth's bloody nose. Dark red blood from the deep gaping cut.

"Who was your team leader?"

"A man called Bleach. He was a good man. Straight-laced. *Very* straight-laced. A little too much if you ask me, but he was always fair. I believe every decision he made was based on getting the job done in the best way. He seemed very aware of his own ego, doing the best he could to account for it while he led us."

The light in the room changed. When Hugh looked up, he saw the canted figure of his dad leaning against the doorway. "What are you two talking about?"

Neither of them replied.

The same disgust he always regarded Hugh with, his dad nodded at James. "I hope you're not filling his head with nonsense about your time on national service? I hope you've told him the truth of it? That it's brutal and sad, and he'll be lucky to come home alive."

Dark red blood. A tight clench to his jaw, Hugh spoke through it. "What I'm telling him is none of your business. If you want to start being a dad rather than a thorn in our family's side, then let us know; otherwise, we don't need your input."

The slightest twist of his head, his lazy green eyes narrowed as they fixed on Hugh. For a moment, he looked like he might offer a spiteful retort. Then the tension fell from his face. After tucking his long ginger hair behind one ear—the atmosphere in the room thickening—the man shook his head and left.

Silence filled the space for a few seconds. James broke it. "There's rumours, you know?"

"Rumours tend to have little value."

"About a boy in the woodwork district."

"You don't go anywhere near that district, you hear me?" Scar tissue. Dark red blood. Leering faces. What had they done to her?

"That he had a run-in with someone from this district. A strong boy with a medal around his neck."

Hugh didn't reply.

"They say an entire gang attacked him. It was the same night you *fell over* when out running. The night you came home covered in bruises. Anyway, they say a gang attacked him, but he managed to get a hold of their leader and his blade. He held the kid at knifepoint while he led him away, forcing the rest to stay put."

Dark red blood. The screams of a teenage boy.

"The boy came back with a star cut into his stomach. A deep cut too. So deep it tore his abdomen and pierced his gut."

Unable to control the shake running through him, Hugh stared at the table. "And the boy? Is he okay?"

"Too early to tell. It doesn't look good though. They just hope he doesn't pick up an infection."

"If he dies, it'll serve him right."

The statement derailed his brother, his mouth hanging half open.

"Just make sure you stay away from those boys, you hear me?"

"Will they hurt me?"

If Hugh could have answered that, he would. Ranger. He looked into his little brother's innocent face. Blood. Had he just condemned him to ten years of hell before he went on national service himself? Lance. Ranger. Elizabeth. Dark blood. Shit. Bile. "You'll be fine."

"How do you know?"

"You'll be fine. Okay?" Anxiety ate away at Hugh's gut, slashing it like the sharp blade of a knife. He had to leave for the trials soon. How could he tell the boy in front of him that everything would be okay? His gut knew the truth of it. He'd just made his brother's life a hell of a lot worse.

CHAPTER 11

Because Spike spent a lot of time outside every day, he felt the changing weather as they moved deeper into winter. The burn in his throat when he ran, the increased size of the clouds of condensation, the quicker he felt the chill when he stood still—which he did now.

It had taken a little bit of digging, which finally ended with him asking one of the retired team leaders in ceramics. Even then, he only found out in which district he could find Bleach. When he got to construction though, he soon found someone who knew the man and where he lived.

The houses in construction were patchwork from where they'd been strengthened and improved upon piecemeal. The repairs gave the properties history. It looked like they'd added to their buildings as they'd discovered new techniques. A district undergoing constant renovation, from the look of the place, Spike would have guessed that far fewer houses collapsed here than anywhere—except perhaps the political district. Influence and power allowed snakes like Robert Mack to be supplied with only the best.

Regardless of the final decision Bleach had made, with everything else that had gone on during his six months of national service, surely he thought fondly of Spike? And he owed him. He should have voted for him. Maybe he'd see this as his chance to address his error. If Spike thought about it for too much longer, he'd stand there all day, so he raised his hand and knocked on the strong wooden door he'd been directed to.

The sound of steps on the other side, the door then pulled open in front of him. The sight of the woman forced Spike back a step. A beautiful woman in her thirties with long blonde hair and bright blue eyes, a fierce intelligence and strong will fixed on him. In a city filled with patriarchs, this woman stood as an equal. As she appraised Spike, he opened and closed his mouth, unable to get his words out.

"Can I help you?" the woman finally said.

"Uh, I think I've come to the wrong house."

"You've knocked on my door to tell me you've come to the wrong house?"

Two children appeared. One boy and one girl, they both had the blonde hair of their mother. They couldn't have been any older than ten. Not only did the girl have her mother's hair, but she had her looks. The boy appeared to be made from thicker stock. For a few seconds, Spike looked at the boy. The uncanny resemblance couldn't be a coincidence. He'd come to the correct house. "Is Bleach in, please?"

The woman pushed the children behind her as if she feared for their safety. "*Who?*"

Heat flooded Spike's cheeks. "Bleach? I'm sorry; I must have got the wrong place."

"Are you from national service?"

The whole interaction had left Spike reeling, and he said it more as a question, as if he didn't even know himself. "Yes?"

"You either are or you're not."

"I am."

"I think you want Dave."

"Dave?"

She didn't say anything else; instead, she turned her back on Spike, shoved the children into the house after they hadn't gone on the first push, and shouted, "Honey, one of your cadets is at the front door."

If the thuds of Bleach's steps were anything to go by, Spike shouldn't have come here. Had he longer to think about it, he would have run, but before he'd had a chance, Bleach filled the doorway and looked him up and down. "What are *you* doing here?"

"Hi, Bleach."

"Dave. I'm not on national service now. What? You think my wife and kids call me *Bleach*?"

"I didn't know you have kids. Although, I would assume they call you Dad."

"Well, I do have kids. Kids that I had to spend six months away from because I was dealing with your nonsense on national service, so don't get smart with me, boy. And I suppose you get people to call you Spike all the time?"

Spike didn't answer.

"It's all bullshit. Surely, you've seen that by now? All the names. The ceremony. It's all window dressing for a badly run construction project with an atrocious safety record."

Spike drifted away for a moment. "I'd not really thought about it before, but why don't they have more guards outside the city to deal with the diseased on national service?"

"You're only just asking that now? Eighteen years on this planet and you're only starting to question these things?" He lowered his voice as if trying to prevent his family from hearing him. "I suppose you still believe in Santa too, right?"

Spike didn't answer.

"We have a shortage of citizens in every district. Besides, the more people we put outside the wall, the more diseased it attracts. Any more than about one hundred protectors out there has diminishing returns. We've tried it in the past and spent most of the time in a war just outside the gates. Anyway, I'm sure you haven't come here to have a candid discussion about how the city runs. And you've deemed it important enough to take me away from my kids, so what do you want?"

Spike's tongue felt too thick for his mouth. He hadn't thought it through. He managed just one word. "Artan."

"What's Artan?"

"Matilda's brother."

"You've not given up on each other yet?"

"I'm still in the trials. No thanks to you."

"So you've come to moan at me? Besides, you're in the trials against *Ranger Hopkins*."

After drawing a deep breath, Spike said, "Look, I need your help."

"I figured this isn't a social visit. And why would I give it to you?"

"Because you …" He left the sentence hanging.

"Were you just about to say I owe you?"

"No …" Although if the heat in his face looked as bad as it felt, he hadn't hidden the lie very well. "Because you understand what it's like to have a brother who needs help."

The already dark mood darkened, and Bleach appeared to swell, filling more of the doorway as he straightened his back.

"Matilda's dad was violent towards her, her mum, and her brother for years."

"She's not special in that regard. National service screws people over. It breaks lives and ruins families. The city expects them to deal with it behind closed doors. So why should I care?"

"Her dad killed her mum the other week."

Bleach's green eyes remained on Spike, although the skin around the edges of them twitched.

"Her brother fought back and killed her dad."

The facade dropped and Bleach exhaled hard, scratching his head and looking at the ground. "I'm not sure what you want me to do about it?"

"We just want to get visiting rights to him."

"*We?* She ain't going anywhere in the city other than her district. Especially not to go and visit a murderer."

"*I* want visiting rights. It's the first step in getting him out of there."

Bleach shook his head. "It won't happen. You should give up now. This city ain't what they tell you it is. Move on."

"Did you give up on your brother?"

Bleach's words rolled like a landslide, lifting the hairs on the back of Spike's neck. "Careful, William."

The wind taken from his lungs, Spike sagged where he stood.

After a few seconds of silence, Bleach stepped back into his house. "Goodbye. Don't come here again." He closed the door. A second later, the definitive sound of three bolts slammed home on the other side.

CHAPTER 12

Spike emerged from the bathroom with just a towel around his waist to see Matilda at the front door, her neighbour Jan pointing an angry finger at her. The two women stopped mid-argument, and both turned his way. Matilda rolled her eyes while Jan's already puce face turned into a beacon of indignation. "*See?!*" she said, waving her index finger in Spike's direction. "This isn't right."

"There's nothing that says he isn't allowed to be here."

"If you ignore your morals."

"What are you talking about?"

Jan finally dropped her finger and placed her hands on her ample hips. "Do I need to spell it out?"

When Matilda balled her fists, Spike stepped forward. He'd seen this precursor to violence too many times before. She had done it before she knocked Hattie McGraph's front tooth out in primary school, before she drove a kick that sent Duncan Pollark's nuts into his nostrils, and before she landed an uppercut on Jason Mark's chin. It had ruined his reputation as the toughest kid in the school.

Maybe she saw it coming too, because Jan raised her voice.

By drawing attention to their argument, she also drew in witnesses. "You're living like a *whore*! *There*, I said it."

As Matilda lunged forward, so did Spike, his towel slipping from him when he wrapped both his arms around her.

If Jan wanted witnesses, Matilda helped her get them, drawing more attention to their argument, her voice taking flight through the district. "Screw you, Jan. What do you know about anything? You live for idle gossip, you small-minded fool." She twisted against Spike's restraint, his still-wet body giving her lubrication.

But if Jan heard Matilda's torrent of abuse, she didn't react. Instead, she stared at Spike.

The lack of response from her neighbour settled Matilda. A look from Spike to Jan, her face twisted again. "Oh, I see. So you come over here and have the audacity to call me a whore while copping an eyeful of him? Have a good look, why don't ya? You're despicable."

Spike seized his moment and yanked Matilda away from her neighbour, flashing Jan and the district his bare bottom as he kicked the front door closed with his heel.

The wooden barrier between them only did so much to muffle Jan's cry of 'whore', and Spike had to redouble his efforts to stop Matilda charging out into the street for round two. If she got out the front door, she belonged to the guards. He couldn't follow her out in his current state.

Both of them out of breath, Spike grabbed Matilda's shoulders, forcing her to look at him.

Rage-fuelled tears shone in her eyes. "I'm not a whore."

As he took her in, half of her hair loose from the hummingbird clip, Spike smiled, swiped it from her face, and kissed her. "I know."

A knock rapped against the door. Spike let go of Matilda and rushed to his towel. Although Matilda directed her venom at her neighbour by shouting, "Go away, Jan," she let Spike answer it this time.

Where he expected a woman no taller than five feet two inches, Spike stepped back at the size of the man in the doorway. "Bl—Dave?"

The very sight of Spike in a towel looked to be an affront to Bleach. A hard frown hooded his eyes, and he pressed his lips together, the skin around them whitening from the pressure. The pause lasted just long enough to be uncomfortable, but for Bleach to speak before Spike did. "Don't use my brother like that again. I trusted you by telling you what happened with him. If you want something from someone, you should have the courage to ask it outright and accept the answer, even if it's not the one you want to hear."

The cold winter wind bit into Spike's damp skin and he shivered.

"That being said, I've arranged for you to see Artan today. Just *you*." He peered past him at Matilda. "She has to stay in her district. They said they'd let you in when you turn up. Now don't bother me again, okay?"

As Spike opened his mouth to thank him, Bleach turned his back and walked off.

Spike closed the door to be met by Matilda with his clothes in her arms. "*Quick!* Get changed and get over there now!"

CHAPTER 13

A good test of his fitness, Spike made it to the justice department building in record time. As he burst through the front door—the large foyer amplifying his tired breaths—he saw the same receptionist he'd encountered on his previous visit. The place hadn't changed in size, but the gap between the entrance and her desk now appeared to be at least twice the distance. As he walked across the stone floor, his steps echoing, he watched the woman.

When Spike got to within about ten feet of her, the woman finally lifted her head and regarded him with utter contempt.

Spike gulped. "Hi—"

"I think you'd do better to not say anything today."

As much as he wanted to plead his case—to tell her he wasn't a homophobe, that he thought Robert Mack was a despicable human being—it didn't matter what she thought of him. He'd come to see Artan. If she facilitated that, that was all he needed. "Bleach … uh, I mean Dave, I mean Bleach … I dunno what you call him here, but the man who was my team leader on national service came to see someone?"

"Yep."

"They said I can see Artan?"

"Yep." A small bell on her desk, the receptionist picked it up in a two-fingered pinch, her pinkie sticking out as she rang it. Like every other sound in the cavernous foyer, the tinkling started small and swelled to fill the space. While she waited, the receptionist levelled a deadpan stare at the medal around Spike's neck.

It only took a few seconds—but it felt much longer—before a large man and woman appeared from a door behind the reception-ist. They were built like they used to be protectors. They had bulky frames, a layer of cushioning covering their solid mass to show they clearly didn't work out like they used to. Although neither was as tall as Spike, they were both wider—much wider. They stood with relaxed postures, emanating a comfort in their abilities to deal with whatever came their way.

Because the receptionist held on for so long, Spike nearly introduced himself, but just before he could, she said, "This boy's here to see prisoner twenty-two."

As much as Spike wanted to correct her and call him Artan, he didn't. Matilda would have. Maybe that was why he was the better person to come today. It didn't matter what they called him as long as he found a way to get him free.

Again, the two guards watched Spike, and neither moved. The woman finally turned and opened the door she'd just walked through. The man followed her, and Spike took up their tail.

The corridor—low ceilinged and made from exposed brick and rock—stretched both ways. Doors lined the wall opposite, a gap of about eight feet between each one. They were strong wooden doors, and there must have been at least twenty of them. How many had prisoners on the other side?

The man turned left and Spike followed him, the smell of human waste and dirt hanging in the air. He looked at the doors as they passed them. What had the prisoners done to be locked up?

Had any of the others killed someone? How many of them were minors waiting to be old enough to be evicted?

The man finally stopped at a door that looked just like the others. Three heavy bolts ran from the top to the bottom, which he unlocked with three loud cracks that ricocheted through the long corridor. Groans, moans, and shrieks rose from the oppressive atmosphere as if the sound agitated the insanity cooped up in some of the cells. Many of them sounded like they had no idea what they were responding to, as if they'd lost their minds along with their freedom.

The hinges released a yawning groan when the guard opened the door, and Spike winced at what he might see. Had Artan contributed to the deranged chorus?

When Spike walked into the cell, he gasped at the state of the boy. Normally well groomed and fresh faced, his cropped hair had grown out to a thick fuzz, and he fixed his gaze on Spike's feet. The cell smelled worse than the corridor, a ceramic pot in the corner that clearly hadn't been emptied for some time. Yellow foam floated on the brown liquid.

As he took him in, breathing through his mouth, but not covering his nose—as much as he wanted to—Spike was already editing his experience so he could relate it to Matilda. She didn't need to know just how bad her brother looked.

Artan finally lifted his tired gaze, deep bags beneath his eyes.

Spike smiled through his shock and searched the familiar face for the boy he knew. In a few short weeks, he looked to have aged years. He pushed aside his trepidation and said, "Hi, mate."

Bars of white beneath his irises, Artan looked at Spike like he didn't recognise him.

"How are you?"

"Where's my sister?"

"She's not allowed out of ceramics. I had to come on her behalf."

"I want to see her."

"And she wants to see you, but she's not allowed."

Artan slowly returned his attention to the floor.

"We're going to get you out. Everything will be okay."

While tracing the same small circle on the stone floor with his right index finger, Artan said, "I'm not sure how much longer I can keep it together. I've been going out of my mind."

"I can imagine. But we're working on a few things. We'll get you out, I promise."

Artan's defences visibly dropped. He looked at Spike again and, in that moment, returned to being Matilda's little brother. "Do you really think you can get me out?"

What else could he tell the boy? "Absolutely. We're close to it. Things can take a while in this city, but it is happening." They both had to believe in the system. Artan in Edin's justice; Spike in Edin's selection of the next apprentice.

Artan's eyes swelled with tears. "I'm so scared, Spike."

Despite the boy smelling almost as rancid as the pot in the corner, Spike hunched down close to him and leaned forwards so their foreheads touched. "I can only imagine. Just know there are two of us working hard to get you out. Don't lose hope, because we won't. Ever."

Because he couldn't tell him anything more than he already had, Spike wrapped Artan in a hug and let the boy sob.

AT LEAST FIVE MINUTES PASSED WITH THE TWO OF THEM LOCKED together before Spike finally let go of Artan and got to his feet. "Is there anything you want me to say to Tilly?"

"Tell her it was self-defence."

"She knows that."

"Tell her I'm sorry."

"You have no reason to be sorry."

"Tell her I'm depending on her."

She didn't need to hear that. "I'm hoping I can get a couple more visits in before the trials. It's good to see you. Know we'll have you out of here in no time." Whether Spike believed it or not, he had to for both Matilda's and Artan's sakes. Hell, he had to for his own sake. Without hope and faith in the system, none of them stood a chance.

While knocking on the door to be let out, Spike fought to keep it together, his eyes burning with the start of his tears, his vision blurring. Artan didn't need to see him upset, but he needed to make sure he let it out before he returned home to Matilda.

The bolts snapped free on the other side of the door before it opened. As much as Spike should have turned around to say goodbye to Artan, he couldn't. He'd already given him all the hope he had for that day. The spark of negative thought had caught ablaze and was suffocating his mind with its noxious cloud. If they didn't find a way to get him out, Artan could quite conceivably spend the next few years of his life in that small room, pissing and shitting in a bucket while he waited to be evicted from the city.

CHAPTER 14

Maybe Hugh couldn't sleep because he had the trials in the morning. Maybe the images of blood and violence that played on a constant loop through his mind kept him awake. His thoughts of Lance and Ranger. How he remembered Elizabeth, wild with the disease, her arms and legs spasming as it took control of her body. Her cries the moment they morphed into something else, something animal: the distorted and tormented roar of a diseased. It gave an audible indication of her transition from human to one of them. Whatever the cause of his restlessness, the fact remained, he'd been lying on his back in his bed for what felt like hours, and there seemed little chance of him dozing off any time soon.

The bright moonlight shone through Hugh's flimsy curtains. Something he wouldn't normally notice, but tonight it had become an interrogator's spotlight, adding to the white noise of insomnia.

At that time of night, most of the district was at home in bed, the near silence only broken by the occasional shuffling of feet. More often than not, they were the gangs of youths who had no desire for anything other than to survive national service. They were too young to care about tailoring and too old for their parents to force them to stay in. With the mortality rate of national service, why should they think about a life beyond that? Half of them wouldn't ever get to live it. As long as the trouble they got into didn't come back on their family, then who cared? Besides, the kids who went out at night armed with knives and catapults had a good chance of coming home with nocturnal animals. Mostly mice and rats, but they helped bolster each family's austere rations.

As if on cue, Hugh heard something. He strained his ears to listen again, but the sound came from inside his house. From across the hall. From James' room.

The excuse he'd been waiting for, Hugh got out of bed. Any hint of sleep got driven from his body by the cold, late October air as he pulled his clothes on before stepping out into the hallway. He and James had rooms opposite one another. Their parents were at the end of the hall. Now he'd moved closer to his brother's room though, Hugh strained his ears and heard nothing. Maybe he'd imagined it. Then what sounded like a stifled gasp whispered at him through the gap beneath his brother's bedroom door.

A glance to the end of the corridor at his parents' room, Hugh then crossed to his brother's, gently knocked on the door, and let himself in.

James stood in just his pants, the skinny boy shock white and shivering, his face sodden with tears.

"What's up?" Hugh said.

While biting his bottom lip, James looked down at his lap.

"Have you had an accident?"

James nodded.

Without another word, Hugh left his brother's room, returning a few minutes later with the sheets and duvet from his own bed.

While wrapping his skinny arms around himself, James said, "Wh … what are you going to sleep in?"

"I'll take your bedding."

"But it's soaked."

"Let me worry about that."

"Aren't you worried what Dad will say to you?" James took on a mocking version of his dad. "*You're too old to be pissing the bed. Are you a little girl? What's wrong with you, boy?* You've heard how he goes off."

"Screw Dad. I don't care what he thinks. Besides, I won't be here after tomorrow anyway."

Although he didn't move to help him, almost as if he felt ashamed to even touch his wet sheets, James spoke through stuttered sobs. "Thank you."

AFTER HE'D FLIPPED THE MATTRESS, CHANGED THE SHEETS, AND got his brother tucked back in again, Hugh sat on the edge of his bed. He stared at the innocent face of his little brother and wiped his hair from his forehead. "Better?"

Tears still in his eyes, James nodded.

"You don't look it."

"I'm scared, Hugh."

"Is that why you had an accident?"

"Yeah."

"Of what?"

"Of what'll happen to me when you're gone. Of the gangs in the woodwork district. Of Lance."

The thought of dark red blood belched from a deep wound in Hugh's mind. After shaking his head, he got his thoughts back on track. "What do you know about Lance? What's he said to you?"

James cried freely again. "That you'll only be here to look after me for so long. That I'll have to fight for myself while you're losing the trials to Ranger."

"But I'll be back."

"He said a lot can happen in five months."

Elizabeth's arms and legs spasming. Lance and Ranger standing over her. Her bloody nose. What did they do to her behind that wall?

"Hugh?"

Another shake of his head to pull his attention back to the room, Hugh said, "Sorry. I was thinking."

The tears had left James' eyes, which were now narrowed as he appraised his brother, his head tilted to one side. "You've not been the same since you came back from national service."

The lie raced to the edge of Hugh's mouth, but he stopped it dead. The kid knew. Why pretend he felt okay? "It's a hard time on national service. A lot happens and it takes its toll."

"Like it did with Dad?"

"No! Nothing like with him. I'm *not* him."

James pulled his new duvet up so it covered the bottom half of his mouth, and he said, "Please don't bottle up how you feel."

"You sound like Mum."

"She's right. Dad doesn't believe in talking about how he feels, and look what it's done to him."

Hugh bit back his initial reaction. It took the fire from his words and he spoke with a soft tone. "I'm not Dad."

As he looked from one of Hugh's eyes to the other, James said, "I don't know what you need to do to feel better, and I know you're not Dad, but you're not the brother I knew either. I miss him."

Were Hugh not already sitting down, his brother's words would have taken his legs from beneath him. After he'd drawn a deep breath to try to ease the stabbing pain in his chest, he nodded. "I miss me, too. Look, James, I want you to trust me with something."

The skin at the sides of James' eyes pinched. "What?"

"*Nothing's* going to happen to you while I'm away."

"But—"

"*Nothing!* You hear me?"

James nodded.

"Then I'll be back and we can be a normal family."

"Will we finally get to meet Elizabeth?"

Ranger's sneering grin punched through Hugh's thoughts. "Yeah. You're going to love her. Now get some sleep. Everything's going to be okay. And while I'm away, I'll make sure I find your brother and bring him back with me, okay? Sorry if I've been a bit distracted; I just need time to work some things out. I love you, mate."

"I love you too."

After kissing his brother's forehead, Hugh stood up and left the room.

CHAPTER 15

Matilda's tossing and turning had kept Spike in a state of half sleep for most of the night. When she finally sat up, dragging the covers with her and exposing him to the cold air in the room, it drove away any hope of rest. A candle burned beside the bed, animating the shadows around them, making a gargoyle's mask of her tired face. In Edin, anyone falling asleep with a naked flame still lit could be punished by eviction—the risk of fire was too great. But Matilda hadn't slept for days and didn't appear to be close to it any time soon. Swiping her hair back from her face, she said, "Your mum must hate me by now."

Spike stared at his love. Her eyes were bloodshot, and her skin had grown paler as if the past month had drained the life from her and continued to drain it. "Mum knows I need to be here. She understands."

When Matilda regarded him with a raised eyebrow, Spike thought about the several heated conversations he'd had with his mum over the past few weeks and shrugged. "She *will* understand. Besides, whatever happens, I'll be spending time with her after the trials. We know very few things for sure, but one of them is that I'll be able to go to the agricultural district when all's said and done."

The flickering flame found the glaze in Matilda's eyes as they lost focus for a second before she said, "And he said nothing to you?"

Since he'd come back from visiting Artan earlier that day, they'd been over it plenty of times already, but Matilda needed to hear it again. "Nothing that made sense, no."

"What, he just …?"

As much as he wanted to lie to her, Spike went back to his visit to the justice department's building. He returned to the moment where he watched the boy trace a circle on the floor. "He's not doing well, Tilly."

A fresh wave of tears ran down her cheeks, leaking from her unblinking eyes. The only time Spike had seen colour in her skin came with the red blotches her grief lifted on her face.

The thought had been churning inside Spike for a few days now. With just a couple of hours before he got a carriage to the trials, he had to say it. "Shall I stay?"

When Matilda looked at him, her eyes shifting from one of his to the other, she worked her mouth but clearly couldn't speak.

His stomach sank and it took a great will to continue. "I'll stay; we'll work it out."

"*No!*" She looked at her lap and sighed. "There's no point."

Spike reached across and stroked her back. He'd spent over three weeks living with her. He wasn't looking forward to sharing a room with Hugh, Ranger, and James Swank, not now that he'd had this. "I *want* to be with you. More than anything."

"I want you to be with me too, but you won't be if you don't go on the trials. You'll be forced into agriculture and I'll be here. Forever. You won't be able to visit Artan, and we won't see each other. As much as I don't want you to go away, staying makes no sense."

"I could sneak over here to be with you at night."

"You might get away with that for a short while, but it's not a permanent fix. You think Jan will keep her mouth shut when she sees you coming and going? And you've seen what this city does to people who break the rules."

"I want to be with you while you're going through this."

"I want to be with you *forever*, Spike, and the only way for that to happen is for you to smash these trials. It's going to be a hard five months, but Artan has a few years before he's old enough to be evicted, and as much as I don't want to leave him in that cell—especially in his current state—we have a whole host of bad options in front of us, and I'd say this is the best of the lot."

There seemed little point in arguing, as he had no better case to make. While sitting up, Spike pulled her in close and kissed the top of her head, breathing in her floral scent, saving the memory of it. "This is the final stretch. We've made it here, so there's no reason why we can't go all the way. I've trained as hard as I can. I'll fight for longer and with more force than any other cadet there. I'll give it everything I have."

After she'd released a stuttered sigh, Matilda's voice broke when she said, "I know you will. I know."

CHAPTER 16

The early morning streets were empty, and Hugh's nose and cheeks were already numb from exposure to the cold air. As he ran, his thoughts cycled, returning to the most powerful memory of all: Elizabeth and her bloody face. No matter how many times he relived the memory, the one thing he couldn't get away from was that he could have saved her. Had he been braver, she'd still be alive, regardless of what Ranger and Lance had done. Had he not been wallowing in the loss of his love, he could have made sure Max and Olga's weapons were fine so Max could have gone to the trials like he'd dreamed of doing. Two people's lives had already been ruined because of his inaction; he had to make sure the same didn't happen to his brother.

It was still dark from the sun buried behind the horizon, but Hugh didn't need to see all that well because he knew exactly where he'd be. In just over three weeks, he'd already learned his patterns. And now, for once, he'd make sure he acted accordingly.

When Hugh rounded the next corner, his heart rate quickened to see him standing there. The long and skinny silhouette of Lance. And he stood alone. The boy would no doubt be busy on an apprenticeship in the tailoring district during the day, but he still came out at night. Maybe he couldn't let go of his aspirations to be in the woodwork gangs, to matter to someone, to rule others even though he had nothing to offer anyone. Too stupid to lead, too old to have freedom of movement, he could be a liaison between districts and nothing else.

As he closed down on the boy, Hugh heard the memory of Elizabeth's scream from when she turned. A tight clench of his jaw, he sped up towards the lanky streak of piss.

Because Hugh made no effort to hide his approach, his steps slamming against the cobblestones, Lance looked up at him when they were still separated by at least thirty feet of shadowed alley-way. The tall boy snorted a laugh. "What are *you* doing here?"

Twenty feet between them, Lance stepped away from the wall, his elbows moving away from his sides, his fists balled. Maybe a few months ago, the boy might have stood a chance, but the Hugh that would have yielded to him had been left behind with the corpse of his love and Max's hope of being a protector.

Ten feet between them. The deep cut in the kid from the woodwork district. Thick blood spewing from the dark red wound. The way he screamed when the knife cut his flesh.

Five feet.

A gang of boys stepped through the gap in the wall. Seven or eight of them, they spread out behind Lance.

"Not so sure of yourself now, are you, boy?" Lance and the gang around him laughed. They laughed like Lance and Ranger had. "What? You think we were just intimidating James for fun?"

"Don't use his name, you scumbag."

"Although, we do have plans for Jimmy, but this was about getting you here. We laid the bait and you've gobbled it up. Remember when you were smart? You'd have seen this set-up from a mile off."

"I don't care how many of you there are."

The shuffling of steps behind him, Hugh turned around to see another seven or eight boys.

"You still don't care?" Lance said.

The scream. Blood on her face. Her changing into a diseased. Ranger and Lance's laugh. Lance's laugh. He'd heard it too many times already. No time for talking, Hugh turned one hundred and eighty degrees and charged those closing in from behind.

Hugh released a shrill caw, avian in its hellish staccato. The boys froze long enough for him to reach the one at the front. He crashed into him with his balled fist, a wet crunch where knuckles met cartilage.

The boy let out a cry and held his nose as he went down.

Two closed in on Hugh from either side. Olga had taught him plenty, the main thing being that fighting had just one rule: to win. Fair fights were officiated and held in rings. Do whatever it took in the street.

The muscles in Hugh's legs bulged with coiled power. He kicked one of the boys in the nuts. The force of it lifted the kid from the ground, dropping him a second later. The next one had stepped close enough for him to punch him on his right cheek, snapping the kid's head to one side with a loud *clop*. He folded like his two friends before him.

Three down, Hugh charged the remaining four, meeting the next one with a flying kick to his chest. These kids had relied on numbers to intimidate for too long. They knew nothing about fighting.

The last three ran, and as he watched them away, Hugh panted ragged breaths. His fists still clenched, he turned to face the kids from the woodwork district—except they weren't there.

Lance raised his hands, showing Hugh his palms by way of submission. "Look, man, it wasn't my idea."

Hugh walked towards him. "*You* were the one who told James what you'd do to him. *You* were the one who hurt Elizabeth. *You* were Ranger's lapdog."

"I'm sorry, okay?"

"And where is he now? Although he can move through the districts, I bet you haven't heard from him, have you?" The images of the diseased. Of Elizabeth. Of the wound he cut into the boy in woodwork. They all smashed through his mind, each one making him flinch and nearly derailing his thoughts, but his purpose was too strong to be sidetracked. "I'm going to the trials tomorrow. I need to ensure *nothing* happens to James."

"It won't, I promise."

"And you think your promise is worth something to me?"

"I'll make sure he's okay."

"I know you will." Just a few feet separated them, Hugh continuing to close him down. "You want to know how I know that?"

Lance didn't reply, stepping back as Hugh came forward.

"Because I'm going to make sure of it. I'm going to give you a taste of the consequences should *anything* happen to him. You've pushed people around for too long. The entire district needs to see you for the spineless arsehole you are."

The glint of Lance's blade caught the light. It gave Hugh enough of a warning and he jumped back, Lance swiping air with his attack. Before he had a chance to go for him a second time, Hugh kicked the back of Lance's hand and watched his weapon fall to the cobblestones.

Dark red blood. Ranger's face. Hugh charged, knocking Lance to the ground with one punch. As he fell, Hugh followed him down, landing over him. "You pushed me and pushed me!" He slammed his forearm against Lance's nose and felt it burst beneath his blow.

"You killed her!" He smashed him again.

"The only thing stopping me from killing you right now is I need someone to dedicate the next five months to looking after James. When I come back, I'll decide if you've done a good enough job." After he'd driven another blow against his face, Hugh watched Lance's lazy eyes roll back in his head.

Hugh slapped Lance so hard it stung his palm. It did the job, bringing the boy's consciousness back. "Tell me James will be protected."

Before Lance could say anything, Hugh punched him again. "Say it."

It looked like it took him a great effort to get his words out, his mouth filled with blood, his nose flattened. "He'll be—"

Hugh punched him again, grabbed his shirt by the lapels, and lifted him from the ground before slamming him down. "Say it."

Lance cried and shook, his words muffled, blood spraying from his mouth. "I'll make sure he's okay."

Hugh punched him again. "This is only the beginning for you." Another punch, his right fist stinging from the assault he rained down on the boy. "I'm going to watch you for the rest of your *life*. If you ever fall in love with someone, I'll *kill* them. You understand me?"

Although Lance looked like he wanted to reply, Hugh drove another forearm across his face. Panting, he got to his feet and repeated, "I'll kill them," while driving a hard kick into Lance's stomach. "I'll kill them! I'll kill them!" He delivered each threat with another blow, Lance gasping as he lay on the ground in a pool of his own blood. He saw Elizabeth in his mind. Her twitching death. Her changing into one of the diseased.

While yelling, Hugh delivered one final kick, driving the laces of his boots into Lance's face.

Lance fell limp.

After wiping his tears away, Hugh stood over the unconscious form of his tormentor and whispered, "I'll kill them," before turning his back on the boy and walking away. In a few hours' time, he'd be starting the trials. He'd be sharing a dorm with Ranger. What he'd just done to Lance was merely practice.

CHAPTER 17

"Only six competitors this year!" Sarge yelled through his loud hailer, the metal cone pressed to his lips. The crowd of hundreds were silent, hanging on his every word. He nodded in Spike's direction before adding, "We nearly had just five."

Spike had never felt so small as he stood in the line of six with the other competitors, the attention of so many people boring into him. Since he'd arrived back at the training area, one of the new team leaders took his bags while another rushed him to the ring to join the other five. They didn't blame him for arriving last, because he couldn't control when his carriage collected him, but it didn't change the fact that everyone had to wait. It didn't make his entrance any less of a spectacle. And now this: Sarge digging him out in front of an arena filled with spectators by both reminding him, and telling them, of his past failures. Heat flooded his cheeks, but he said nothing.

Sarge hobbled as he walked up and down in front of the trainees, the muddy ground squelching beneath his steps. "As always, we promise these games will be harder, faster, and more violent than any you've seen before. Whoever wins the next apprenticeship will have to sweat blood for it."

A reflection of his own apprehension in the faces of most of the other cadets, Spike looked down the line until he got to Hugh at the other end. The one he'd expected to be the most nervous, the boy clenched his jaw and stared back at the audience as if issuing them an open challenge. Whatever had happened to him during his month away, the scared boy from national service had been shed like dead skin: stockier, braver, and from the look of him, more determined.

"We've been working on these trials for months now, and we can't wait to show them to you," Sarge continued.

Did he have children like Bleach—Dave—did, or did Sarge spend his entire life in the national service area? Maybe they didn't offer him time off on account of not having to go beyond the wall. He'd hardly earned it.

Sarge introduced the competitors, starting with Hugh. "He may look like a lab rat, but this boy has come on so much in the past six months, and looking at him now, he might even stand a chance of winning the trials. Hugh Rodgers!"

Spike joined the others in looking down the line at his friend. His expression remained unchanged, his attention still fixed on the crowd.

"James Swank. He did well to keep his head when many around him lost theirs. A calm and composed candidate who should go far."

It looked like James tried to follow Hugh's lead, although his brooding glare gave off the appearance of a child rather than a competitor. Maybe he realised it, because he lifted a limp hand and waved instead.

Despite the tall bleachers encircling the arena, the wind still blew strong enough to throw Fran Jacob's curly brown hair into her face. She did nothing to prevent it as Sarge introduced her. "One of the smartest cadets in training, what she lacks in speed and muscle, she more than makes up for with guile: Fran Jacobs."

The crowd had remained quiet to let Sarge speak, but then he got to Ranger. In the month they'd been away, and because he'd had so many other things to think about, Spike had wondered if his hatred for the boy had diminished. However, as he looked at him now, his heart hammering, he balled his fists, desperate to throw them into his thick face. As if backing him up, the crowd booed.

"He can't hold a flame to his dad, but then who can? The protector's son: Magma's boy."

Again, Ranger looked as if he tried to mimic Hugh, but Spike saw in his wince that Sarge's introduction hurt. He came into the trials as the favourite. On top of that, he had to carry the weight of his dad's legacy, and Sarge hadn't even named him. Hopefully, he'd buckle from the pressure.

It took about thirty seconds for the crowd to quieten down, and as Spike looked at the red jeering faces, his legs shook. One person away from being introduced, and then after that, he'd have to perform in front of them for the trials. Even worse, he'd have his loved ones watching on. What if he made a total fool of himself?

"I'll be honest with this one." Sarge looked Liz up and down. "I'm not sure why she's here other than to make up the numbers."

Clearly still pumped from Ranger's introduction, the crowd laughed.

"Maybe she'll surprise us all. Liz Barber."

A low blow, Spike watched Liz turn as red as her hair. When Sarge closed down on him, his stomach flipped, his palms sweating.

"Now this one wasn't my choice."

Spike glared at Sarge.

"But this here is the second-chance kid. The rule breaker. Romeo, risking his life to save his lover. It's just a shame he's not the favourite to get through this, because he'll never see her again when all's said and done. William Johnson."

Spike looked out at the crowd, and his stomach continued to turn backflips. As much as he wanted to react to Sarge's goading, it would do him no favours.

"One last time, ladies and gentlemen, boys and girls, please give it up for our six candidates."

This time, the crowd erupted, the sound hitting Spike in a wave that felt like it could burst his eardrums. Disorientated and dizzy, it wasn't until one of the new team leaders grabbed Spike's arm that he saw they wanted to lead him away. While leaving the ring, passing over a wooden hatch in the ground, he watched the crowd. Whatever else happened, he'd have to get used to them.

IT TOOK FOR THE TEAM LEADER—A WOMAN NO MORE THAN FIVE feet six inches tall but with biceps as thick as Spike's thighs—to lead them to their dorm before anyone spoke. It seemed futile to try to communicate over the noise coming from the arena. The team leader pointed at the room on the left and said, "Boys." She then indicated the room on the right. "Girls."

Spike pointed at the room in the middle. "Who's in there?"

"Sarge." Before anyone could ask her any more questions, the fierce woman left.

If the looks on the faces of the other cadets were anything to go by, all of them had found the experience overwhelming—all of them save Hugh. The boy had the same dark look in his eyes, and he currently had his glare fixed on Ranger.

James Swank led the way into the boys' dorm while the two girls walked into theirs. He turned to face the others as they came in and said, "Everyone here calls me James—which I really hate;

only my mum calls me James—because we're going to be together for a while, can you all please call me Jamie?"

Spike and the other two boys shrugged. "Sure," Spike said as he looked around the room. Similar to the one he'd stayed in when they were in team Minotaur, it had little more than two bunk beds in the plain wooden space.

Hugh walked over to one of them and threw his bag on the bottom bunk.

When no one else moved, Spike went to his friend and claimed the bed above him. Waiting for someone to say something, he relaxed to see Ranger and James accept the other bunks.

"Look," Ranger said.

While fixing on the boy, Spike felt Hugh tense beside him. The air damn near crackled from his emanation of pure wrath. Not for the first time, Spike looked at his friend. He had muscles that weren't there four weeks ago. His eyes were sunk much deeper into his skull, ringed with dark shadows. His thick hands were balled into fists, his knuckles cut and swollen. What had happened to him?

Ranger looked at Hugh, his mouth half-open. After a few seconds, he said, "I want to say sorry. I was an arse during national service. I lost my shit because of the pressure. What you saw wasn't me."

Words he'd never expect to hear from the arrogant prick, Spike watched him, all three of them letting him continue.

"I just want you all to know I'm here to compete. Of course I am. But I want to win this fair and square, as I'm sure you all do. I won't be the cause of any drama. I'm here to get my head down and get on." He held his hand in Jamie's direction. They shook.

When he did the same to Spike, Spike paused for a moment. He finally took the boy's hand and looked into his eyes. The nasty kid from national service appeared to have left him. Maybe the situation had screwed him up like he said. Maybe he didn't need to understand or care why he behaved how he did. As long as he kept to himself, what did it matter?

Ranger walked over to Hugh and offered him his hand. "I'm sorry for everything that's gone on."

The same tension in the air, Spike could have sworn he heard the fizz of an electrical current as the two boys locked stares. Although, the aggression only went one way; Ranger was uncharacteristically submissive.

Instead of shaking his hand, Hugh turned his back on the boy and unpacked his bag.

Back to Spike, Ranger said, "And I wanted to tell you how much I respect you."

"For what?"

"For not telling me about my dad coming second the year he did the trials. You knew about that all along, didn't you?"

Spike nodded.

"You're a class act. Many people would have been dragged into my nonsense and struck some low blows. You kept your integrity."

The words and demeanour of the boy he despised utterly derailed Spike, and he offered no reply as he watched Ranger go to his bed on the bottom bunk and unpack his things. Maybe the trials wouldn't be as stressful as he'd anticipated. Then he turned to Hugh again and watched the boy for several seconds. Maybe he'd anticipated drama from the wrong person.

CHAPTER 18

Despite all the chatter around him, Hugh shut it out, focusing on folding his top and stuffing it into the small shelf space that had been allocated to him for his clothes. Storage had been limited when there were three of them in Minotaur's dorm. Now they needed to fit four into the same space. It left him with the challenge of squeezing everything he'd brought into one cubic foot.

Even folding clothes proved difficult with his cut and swollen hands. Hugh clenched his teeth as every action sent a throbbing pain up his forearms, but the sensation also reminded him James would be okay. Lance's pulped face flashed through his mind. The boy's eyes had been swollen to slits before he'd left him, the moonlight making the blood on his face glisten. What must he have looked like this morning? Who found him? Did they even care? The vile shit got what he deserved.

Hugh picked up a pair of trousers and folded them next. His thoughts went from the blood coming from Lance's nose to the last time he'd seen Elizabeth, her top lip crimson from whatever they'd done to her behind that wall. It didn't matter how he wanted to remember Lance, his mind always returned to him and Ranger laughing at the demise of the girl he'd fallen for.

As Hugh forced in more clothes, his hand scraped against the shelf above. It made his fingers twitch and spasm from the electric jabs running through them.

It took for another person to enter the room for Hugh to break away from his work. When he turned to see Sarge in the doorway —the rough vet staring disgust at the cadets—he waited for the man to speak.

"Lunch in ten minutes, boys." Fran and Liz stood behind him.

Although Spike, Jamie, and Ranger left the room, Hugh remained so he could finish unpacking. A job almost complete would drive him mad, and Sarge said they had ten minutes. In the room on his own, he dragged another top from his bag, breathing in through his nose as he folded it. The muscles in his upper body tensed as he relived the beating he'd handed to Lance. The crunch of bone beneath skin. The grind of pulped cartilage. The boy would look different forever because of his beating. It would help him remember the time when he stuck his neck out too far.

Where Hugh had been oblivious to the background noises when the boys were in the room, the squeaky floorboard in the corridor outside went off like an alarm. He turned in time to watch Ranger enter.

Although Ranger smiled, his dark eyes didn't. Even when pretending to be happy, he clearly couldn't shake his sardonic sneer. "Look, man, I think we got off on the wrong foot."

The muscles in Hugh's body locked when Ranger stepped closer. The threat of a shake started beneath the surface as images assaulted his mind. Blood belching from a deep wound. The diseased. Ranger's sneer. Lance. Elizabeth.

Ranger led with his hand again. "Come on, man. Let's shake on it and move on, yeah?"

A deep, gaping cut. Punches rained down on a smug face.

Screams and cries as Lance took a beating on his way to being battered unconscious.

"I wasn't myself over the past few months."

Elizabeth turning into a diseased. Her twitching limbs.

No more than a foot separating them now, Ranger glanced down at Hugh's clenched fists before looking him in the eye again. He smiled. "You don't need to cry. I'm not going to hurt you."

The sting of tears, Hugh clenched his jaw hard as if it would help him keep everything contained.

"I've said I'm sorry."

When Hugh didn't reply, a flicker disturbed Ranger's facade, the change in his expression emanating from his sneer outwards. A ripple of poison that started small until it owned his face. "Spike would have done better, you know?"

It snapped Hugh back into the present moment.

"He would have saved Elizabeth. He's a hero. He wouldn't have run back with his tail between his legs."

The knife going into the boy in woodwork's stomach. Deep red blood.

"Were you anywhere near as brave as him, you would have made sure the girl you loved survived. But you were too busy looking after yourself, weren't you?"

The swelling on the back of Hugh's hands throbbed with a heavier pulse than before. The tension of his tight grip ran up his forearms, and he shook, his world blurring with his tears.

"There's no use in crying, boy. That won't help. But I can give you a piece of advice that will." Ranger then moved so close their faces were almost touching. "You'd best sleep with one eye open from here on out. I'm going to make your pathetic little life hell in these trials. I'm going to ruin you."

The same creaking floorboard in the hallway, Ranger looked over his shoulder as Spike walked into the room, his face returning to the one he'd worn when apologising to them. "Spike! Are you okay?" A flick of his head in Hugh's direction, he said, "Hugh and I were just chatting, trying to clear the air, you know?"

Despite Ranger's words, Spike didn't look like he'd fallen for them, keeping his attention on Hugh and remaining in the doorway while Ranger left the room.

The fire died down. Deep red blood. Elizabeth. Lance. Ranger. The diseased. The shake slowly left Hugh. He didn't know how many times Spike had tried to say it already, but from his tone, it didn't sound like the first time. "Hugh? Hugh?"

"Uh …"

"Is everything okay?"

Hugh nodded. "Yeah." He laughed. "Fine; why wouldn't it be?"

"What did Ranger say?"

"He's trying to connect with me. I'm just not ready for it, you know?" The deep belching wound punched through his mind. Twitching limbs.

"I know, mate. Come on, let's go and eat, yeah?"

The last top from his bag, Hugh folded it and shoved it into a space it had no right fitting into. It scraped the back of his hands again and made his eyes water more than before, another round of spasms snapping through his fingers. Before turning to Spike again, he rubbed his eyes, sniffed a wet sniff, and followed his friend from the room.

CHAPTER 19

S pike's stomach bucked as he threw up his breakfast on the muddy ground. The crowd roared with laughter while he stretched his mouth wide to help him breathe. It might have seemed like a cruel reaction, but the spectators were there to be entertained. The cadets were on their fifth lap, and they'd not yet given the audience a reason to get excited.

The path around the outside of the arena ran a circuit of about eight hundred feet. Not very far on its own, but enough when in front of packed stands, and when added to the tasks they had to do in the centre between laps. Hugh ran ahead of everyone, Ranger behind him, and Spike next. Throwing up had helped him clear the lump in his stomach. He'd eaten too much that morning.

A look behind at Fran, Liz, and Jamie, Spike saw red faces and tired gaits that reflected his own lethargy. Liz and Jamie appeared worse than Fran, glowing like beacons—although, most of that could have been on account of their pale complexions. Even Ranger in front of him looked to be struggling, stumbling occasionally as he squelched through the muddy ground. The only one who appeared in control was Hugh. The pacemaker. The rules of this trial saw cadets eliminated if they were still on their previous lap when the leader completed the three tasks in the centre and started their next run around the ring's perimeter. They were close to that happening, the sound of the spectators rising with their excitement.

Still over one hundred feet to go, Spike gasped as he watched Hugh start the challenges in the centre for the sixth time. The boy wore a fixed expression as he ran to the first task. Lumps of grey rock like Spike had seen in the fallen city, they all had metal bars protruding from them, which made them easier to grip, but heavier to lift. Six were lined up in size order, and the first to arrive at them got first choice of which one to pick. Hugh picked up the largest rock again, lifting it over his head as if it weighed nothing.

As Hugh moved on to the next station, Ranger arrived at the first and picked up the smallest lump of rock. In the face of Hugh's strength, it made him look like a coward. The crowd's jeers were so loud, they made Spike's ears ring.

The third one to reach the lumps of stone, even the second smallest sent a violent shake through Spike's arms as he raised it above his head, his eyes stinging beneath a waterfall of sweat. The crowd seemed neither impressed nor annoyed. He scanned the hundreds of faces to try to locate his dad and Matilda. Nothing.

As he reached the second station, Spike watched Ranger run to be with Hugh at the third. Magma's son now moved like a diseased, his tired legs stealing his coordination and threatening to send him crashing to the ground.

Press-ups. Hugh had done five, Ranger ten, Spike had to do fifteen. They did them on the wooden hatch in the centre of the ring. It covered what Spike could only assume to be a pit of some sort. It reminded him of Billy Groves, and as he gritted his teeth, pushing through the pain in his upper body, he imagined the boy banging to be let out.

Moving on to the next station, Spike looked behind to see Liz reaching the rocks. Fran had slowed to a walk, and Jamie lagged behind her.

A skipping rope next, Spike's stomach flipped again. As the third one to it, he had to jump fifty times. Liz would have to do sixty.

Sarge blew his horn to signal the elimination of both Jamie and Fran in response to Hugh moving off into his sixth lap of the arena. The crowd grew louder, helping Spike quicken his pace. Ranger then set off for lap six.

Following the other two, Spike locked into a rhythm and searched the crowd. Still no sign of Matilda and his dad. When he looked back in front of him, he saw Ranger slowing. Throwing up had been the best thing to happen to him, his stomach lighter, his breathing easier. His target in sight, he quickened his pace.

The same order as before when they reached the lumps of grey rock, although as Ranger lifted his lump to more jeers from the crowd, Spike lifted his just a second later, getting it above his head quicker than Magma's son, so he arrived at the press-ups next. Just ten this time, he busted them out and moved on to skipping, to watch Hugh set off again. The boy didn't have a frame for speed, but his wide waddle spoke of a fierce stamina.

For the second lap in a row, Sarge sounded his horn, eliminating Liz.

Forty skips, Spike set off after his friend before Ranger had even reached the third station.

Now half a circuit behind Hugh, Spike locked onto him and dug deep. The mud tugged on his every step, threatening to drag him to a halt. The cold air bit into his hot skin, and his lungs burned as he fought to fill them.

Less than halfway around, Spike nearly gave up when he watched Hugh run to the first station. No way could he make another lap, but Ranger had only just finished skipping. He saw his friend lift the heaviest rock yet again. The sound of the crowd made him dizzy, all of them behind the unexpected leader.

As Hugh moved from press-ups to skipping, Spike got to the rocks. Ranger hadn't even reached the halfway point on his seventh circuit.

Because of the response Ranger had gotten from the crowd, Spike went for the second smallest rock, the rough stone tearing stinging cuts into his hands.

Ten press-ups, Spike's body shook as he pushed through them. Sarge's horn then elicited the loudest cheer yet. Ranger had been eliminated.

Forty skips, Spike damn near fell into his eighth lap. He nearly gave up until he saw Hugh had slowed to a walk. His hands behind his head, his fingers linked, he looked to be struggling to breathe.

Spike caught up to Hugh. "Are you all right, man?"

Hugh didn't reply. Despite his exaggerated actions showing he couldn't breathe, Spike saw he had more in him. Maybe the crowd did too, because they booed and hissed. But what could he do? Whatever Hugh had in his head, Spike needed to win this; his future happiness rested on being the next apprentice. While passing his friend, he patted him on the back and said, "Sorry, man, I can't wait."

By the time he reached the lumps of rock, Spike saw Hugh had stopped. It sounded like everyone there willed the boy to keep going, but instead, he hunched over and leaned on his knees.

Despite the crowd urging him to go for the largest lump of rock, Spike picked up the second smallest one again, lifted it above his head, and threw it back down with a loud squelch. He did five press-ups and skipped thirty times. Part of him wanted to wait for his friend, and for a moment, he stared at him.

Sarge had his horn raised to his lips as he hissed, "What are you waiting for?"

Spike set off to a chorus of boos and jeers as Sarge blew his horn to eliminate Hugh.

The loud tone rang out over the sound of the surrounding chaos, robbing Spike of what little strength he had in his legs. He fell into the mud, knees first, his entire body rocking with his heavy breaths.

WERE SPIKE NOT STANDING ON THE OTHER END OF THE LINE TO Hugh, he would have asked him why he gave up the lead. The boy had avoided him, choosing to stand next to Ranger of all people as they regrouped. He looked stronger, fitter, and faster than he'd ever seen him. He appeared to have recovered quicker than the rest of them too. It didn't make sense why he'd gas when he did, but he could ask Hugh later. While he had the chance, he scanned the crowd again for Matilda and his dad.

The day before, Spike and the other competitors were told they were allowed to invite two people to come to watch the games. They could be from anywhere in the city, as long as they weren't imprisoned. Even though it would have broken his dad's heart, if he'd have had the chance to get Matilda and Artan together, he would have done it. Instead, he had to hurt his mum's feelings by inviting Matilda and his dad, but he still hadn't located them.

Sarge walked over and grabbed Spike's right wrist. He spoke to him from the side of his mouth. "How you got this is beyond me." While raising Spike's arm in the air with one hand, he pressed his metal cone to his lips with the other, the loud hailer echoing through the arena. "This one didn't go the way I thought it would, but rules are rules. Ladies and gentlemen, boys and girls, please give it up for William Johnson."

A barrage of abuse would have been easier than the suffocating silence. Spike squirmed where he stood, but he still searched the crowd for his loved ones. For the two friendly faces in the sea of hostility.

Tension winding through him, threatening to wring the air from his lungs, he finally saw his love and his dad. When he locked eyes with Matilda, she gave him the slightest smile. He nodded back, his body loosening enough to walk out of the ring at Sarge's behest. It didn't matter what the crowd thought; as far as the trials were concerned, he had one down and four to go.

CHAPTER 20

With the first trial done, Spike wanted nothing more than to go to his bed and lie down—even covered in mud. He could wash later. Sarge had other plans though, leading all six cadets to the gym.

After opening the door, Sarge stood aside. Spike followed Fran and Jamie in, the others behind. The second he saw his dad and Matilda, any thought of returning to his dorm left him with a gasp, and he ran over to them, hugging them both, kissing Matilda and clinging on.

While patting him on the back, Spike's dad said, "Well done. First place."

Spike watched Hugh, who'd gone to be with a woman and young boy. It must have been his brother and mum. "I know, right? But I'm not quite sure how I managed to get it."

Both Spike's dad and Matilda looked over at the stocky boy. Spike's dad said, "It was a strange one. I thought he was going to win it for sure. Did he tell you why he pulled up?"

"I've not had a chance to speak to him yet." Before Spike turned back to Matilda and his dad, he noticed Ranger in the corner of the room on his own. He stood by the heavy red curtain covering the cells that held the sheep and the diseased they'd seen in their first week of national service. They locked eyes, and for a second Spike saw the old Ranger staring back at him.

Ranger then pulled a tight-lipped smile and spoke in a voice loud enough for everyone to hear. "Dad's really busy with the protectors."

It killed the chatter in the room. Where only Spike had looked at him, everyone else now turned his way. A flood of red covered his face before he dropped his focus to the floor and left the gym at a fast march.

"That was odd," Matilda said. "How's it been to share a dorm with him?"

"Surprisingly okay."

"Huh?"

"I know. He apologised on the first day, and he's really making an effort. Don't get me wrong, I still think he's a snake, but as long as he keeps his head down for the entirety of this process, it doesn't matter what I think. It's not like I'll ever see him again once we're finished."

To look at Matilda's pale face sent a pang through Spike, but he didn't want to make her feel uncomfortable by asking how she was doing in front of his dad. Instead, he turned to the man. "How's Mum?"

"She sends her love."

"I'm sorry I didn't ask her to come too. I only had two invites."

"She understands."

Even as his dad said it, Spike felt his attention drifting to Matilda. "Um, Dad, I'm *really* sorry, but do you mind if Matilda and I have a moment?"

If it hurt his dad's feelings, he didn't show it. Instead, he wrapped Spike in a hug and whispered, "Your mum and I are both with you through this. We believe in you."

The reply caught in Spike's throat, so he held on to his dad for a few seconds longer before they separated. "I'll see you next month."

Spike's dad patted him on the shoulder before leaving the gym. After watching him out, Spike turned to Matilda. "So what's been going on?"

Her eyes were already filled with tears, her face buckling, her chin shaking. "The neighbours are being awful."

"Jan?"

"Not just Jan. *All* of them. They're being so nasty now you're not there."

"Have you heard anything more about Artan?"

"How could I? They won't let me leave the district. I go to work, come home, eat, and then sleep. I'm counting down the days until you come back."

"I came first today, so at least that's a start. We can only take this one step at a time. We're closer than we were this morning."

The snap of Sarge's clapping hands cracked through the room, and Spike jumped. "Right, visiting time's over until next month."

Spike stepped forward and hugged Matilda, his mouth close to her ear. "I love you. Stay strong. Everything will be okay. We'll find a way, I promise."

Matilda shook in his arms, nodding her head into his neck.

"Just hang in there, okay?"

As the two separated, Spike held onto her hands. Chaos stared back at him. Four months was a long time for her to hold it together.

CHAPTER 21

Hugh worked better on his own nowadays. Running helped him forget. To lock into the physical and push himself to his limits, it left little room for anything else. It kept the nonsense at bay. But he'd promised Spike he'd wait for him. It had been over two weeks since the first trial, and they'd trained together every day since. Maybe they would have anyway, but Hugh knew his fitness helped push Spike to be better, and he couldn't begrudge him the chance to improve. He had to win the trials, after all.

While stretching outside the dorm, the bitter November air urging him to get running, Hugh waited. Instead of Spike, Ranger and Fran emerged first. They'd been together a lot lately. She laughed at his jokes and batted her eyelids at him. To look at the boy and his fake smile clamped a rock in Hugh's gut. Although, he understood why Fran hung out with him: a future with Ranger meant freedom in Edin whether he won the trials or not. Who wouldn't marry someone for such perks?

The pair laughed as they walked towards Hugh. Maybe Fran didn't see it, but the mirth vanished when he and Ranger made eye contact. The same bitterness he'd always had, it bubbled beneath the surface. He might have convinced the others he'd changed, but he hadn't, and he likely never would.

After they'd passed him, Hugh heard Ranger's voice. "I've forgotten something. I'll meet you in the gym, yeah?"

To watch him approach would give the boy too much respect, so Hugh kept his back to him, remaining focused on their dorm. Tension twisted through his shoulders. He'd left himself open for attack, but he fought against his need to turn around, monitoring the boy through the sound of his heavy steps.

A second later, the muscles in Hugh's neck tightened to feel Ranger's hot breath in his ear. Even with the strong wind, his halitosis smothered him. "Don't think you're going to win this because you got lucky with the first trial. I'd had a heavy breakfast that morning; otherwise, I would have smashed you. Don't worry; I'm not going to make the same mistake again. You're going to go home a failure, if you're lucky; if I have anything to do with it, you'll finish these trials outside the wall beneath a mound of rocks next to your darling Elizabeth."

Hugh focused on his breaths while violence screamed through his mind. A clenched jaw and clenched fists, he felt the crunch of Lance's nose all over again. He'd gotten away lightly; Ranger wouldn't be so lucky.

"Spike!"

The loud noise snapped Hugh from his thoughts, and he looked up to see Spike walking towards them, Sarge a few steps behind. Although the boy regarded Ranger with narrowed eyes, Spike still dipped a nod at him. "Morning. You all right?"

"Tickety-boo," Ranger said, slapping a hard clap against Hugh's back.

The impact of his open palm stung, the cold morning making it worse. The Hugh of old would have stumbled forward from the impact, but he didn't budge.

After he'd looked between Hugh and Ranger, who ran back to the dorm, Spike said, "Is everything okay?"

Hugh remembered the dark red blood belching from the deep wound and smiled through it. "Yeah, fine. You?"

Spike shrugged. "You ready?"

It took a few steps for the tension to leave Hugh, his movements awkward for several paces as they jogged in the direction of the arena.

They were allowed access to the gym and the arena during the days. Although, the gym was off on Sundays because the national service cadets remained inside the walls. Ranger and the others had taken to spending most of their time in the gym, so Hugh chose to be anywhere but. It already took a great will to tolerate Ranger's bullshit; he didn't have to make it harder for himself. Besides, training in the muddy arena helped with their conditioning.

They ran through the arena's entrance, the ghostly silence of an empty stadium greeting them as they emerged into the vast open space. The place stretched out as a swamp with only the wooden hatch in the centre to break up the sea of mud. The sound of their squelching steps echoed off the eight-foot-high walls between the arena's ground and the front row of seats.

"I still can't get over Ranger," Spike said.

"What do you mean?"

"How different he is."

The crunch of Lance's cartilage. His swollen eyes. His begging for forgiveness.

"Hugh?"

"Oh, sorry. Yeah, I know what you mean. He seems like a different boy, right?"

"Are you okay?" Spike said.

"Why wouldn't I be?"

"You've had a lot happen. I dunno; you seem distant sometimes. Unreachable."

God, he sounded like James. Why did he need to talk? Talking wouldn't bring Elizabeth back. Talking wouldn't help him get his revenge on Ranger. "I'm fine." Before Spike could probe him again, he said, "And no wonder Ranger's such a dick. He had no one come to visit him after the first trial. If he doesn't even have one person to watch him compete, he must have a lonely home life."

"I know, right? A busy protector as a parent. An expectation to live up to a dad who's probably too busy to guide him. Did you know his mum died when he was young?"

"Yeah. That can't be easy on anyone."

If Hugh said any more about Ranger, the poison would spill out. He had to hold onto it. Bottle it up until he could channel it in the right way. He got his breaths under control before saying, "But what about you?"

"Me?" Spike said.

"How are you?"

"You don't want to hear my worries. We all have stresses in here."

"Try me."

"But … with what happened with Elizabeth …"

Her twitching arms and legs. A shake of his head, as much to banish the thoughts as to reassure his friend, Hugh filled his lungs again and locked back into his rhythm. "What happened to her is sad, but please don't feel like you can't talk to me because of it."

"I'm worried about Matilda."

"Thank you," Hugh said.

"Thank you?"

"It's been two weeks since you saw her. I've been waiting for you to tell me about it."

They'd found a rhythm, their feet slamming down against the muddy ground.

Spike said, "She's not in a good way."

"Do you think you'll get Artan out of prison?"

As they started their third lap, Spike expelled a large cloud of condensation, steam coming from his head, his dark skin glistening with sweat. "I don't know. I really don't. All I can do is try to win the apprenticeship. I'm more use to her with the freedom of the city than trapped in agriculture. Not that I'm asking you to let me win …"

"I didn't think you were."

Their conversation halted for a few seconds. What could Hugh say to him? He'd come here with plans too. Plans he had no intention of sharing.

"I lived with Tilly for the month before we came here."

"How was it?"

"Wonderful. Amazing. But I wish I hadn't."

Instead of replying, Hugh watched his friend wince.

"It just means I now know what I could lose. I've tasted life with her and I might never get to have it again."

"You'll be okay."

"That's easy to say …"

"You'll be okay. Don't worry about it. Keep your head down. Keep training, and you'll be fine. Everything will work out."

"Can I ask you something?" Spike said.

"Sure."

"Why did you play the first trial like you did?"

"What do you mean?"

"You made it harder for yourself by lifting the heaviest rock every time."

"I need the training."

"I'm not sure you do. I haven't seen anyone here who's fitter than you. How did you improve so much during your month off?"

Lance's swollen eyes. The boy in the woodwork district. "I dunno. I just changed what I focused on, you know? Worked harder and decided to put my mind towards winning. We all have voices in our heads. Demons that tell us we should stop. I've learned to turn them off."

"You still haven't answered my question."

"That's because you haven't asked it."

"Why did you throw away the first trial? You should have won."

"I gassed. You had more stamina than me. I thought you'd be happy about the win."

"I am. But what are you up to?"

"I'm trying my best, Spike. Give me a break, yeah? You focus on getting back to Matilda, and I'll focus on what I'm doing."

The conversation died between them, and Hugh felt Spike look across at him, but he didn't look back. Part of him wanted to smile. If his plan worked, Spike would be just fine and Ranger would get exactly what he had coming to him.

CHAPTER 22

"Where are you taking me?" They'd bound Spike's hands so tightly, the cord cut into his wrists. The hood over his head reeked of dust. The motes embedded in the fabric made it hard to breathe. Panic at being led blind also wound his chest tight. When he and Matilda were younger, she'd persuaded him to put his faith in her by falling back into her arms. They must have been ten at the time. It seemed like a good idea. She dropped him. Since then he'd struggled with exercises of trust.

The strong grip on his right shoulder must have belonged to a team leader or guard. They said nothing as they either shoved or dragged him, depending on where they wanted him to go. The muddy ground squelched beneath their steps, and he heard the sound of the crowd in the arena. The tight entranceway condensed the cheers, screams, and abuse. All of it swirled into a dizzying wall of noise, and it felt like his brain would burst.

Even over the sound of the spectators, as Spike entered the ring, he heard the gates to the arena being closed and bolted. Sweating, his throat dry, he fought to pull dusty air into his lungs. What the hell were they planning on doing to them?

It had been muddy on the way over, but now inside the arena,

Spike walked over sludge, his feet twisting with every step while the hungry ground tried to steal his boots. His head spun and his ears rang as he followed the direction of his guide.

After what felt like a lifetime, Spike's leader clapped their other hand on his shoulder, turned him slightly, and backed him into a wall he assumed to be the one running around the arena's perimeter. Now closer to the crowd, their noise gained definition and he heard what some of them had to say. It ran from encouragement to death threats. Neither was helpful, so he shut them out again.

The loud and prolonged toot of Sarge's horn both silenced the crowd and made Spike jump. His ears rang as much with the absence of noise as they had when it had been full volume. His pulse quickened as he listened to his own breaths in the confined space of his hood.

The loud hailer did such an effective job of projecting Sarge's voice, Spike wondered if they heard it in Edin. Despite the distance between them, he imagined his mum straining her ears across the miles separating them. "Ladies and gentlemen, boys and girls—if that's even necessary; whoever brings their kids to something like this needs their heads checked."

The crowd remained almost silent, only a small section laughing at the poor gag.

"Today's trial is quite simple. Last cadet standing wins."

Spike's stomach clenched. What were they about to do to them?

"You get knocked down and you're out. *Guards!*"

The strong grip left Spike's shoulders and grabbed the top of his thick hood.

"In three," Sarge said, "two … one!"

A rush of light hit Spike almost as hard as the sound in the tunnel had. Blinded for a few seconds, he blinked repeatedly in an attempt to regain his sight. A wall of watery colour materialised in the stands. Then he saw what waited for them in the arena.

Several guards stood in the centre by the hatch covering the pit. A weapons rack stood beside them. Before Spike had more than a few seconds to process it, the guards pulled the wood free. Instead of Billy Groves climbing out after all these years, diseased spilled from the hole like wasps from a nest.

The creatures' shrieks emerged with them. Spike looked around the outside of the ring to see the other cadets were like him: frozen and bound.

All limbs, the diseased fell over one another as they tried to clamber to their feet. When they came up covered in mud, they looked worse than ever; as if the ground had birthed them. An uncoordinated charge, they ran on the edge of their balance, fanning out to get to the cadets, who had been equally spaced around the perimeter.

It took just one tug against his bonds for Spike to accept they were too tight. He needed another plan. He looked at the weapons again, but before he could make a decision, Liz burst to life. Her face streaked with tears, she screamed and ran for the rack.

Spike watched on as she drew the diseased to her. She side-stepped the first, sending it crashing down in the mud, but the second one hit her so hard the crowd gasped. In a matter of seconds, bodies smothered her, hiding her from view.

Still in the same spot, Spike's throat drier than ever, he watched the guards from the middle charge to Liz's aid. They lifted the diseased from her. Only then did he see the leather muzzles covering their mouths. And a good job too because they still had their teeth, the click of enamel signalling their despera-tion to drive the disease into their prey's blood. One of the guards led Liz away while the others kicked the creatures, dispersing them so they charged the vulnerable cadets. They seemed able to make the decision between an exposed cadet and armed guard. They knew who the weaker target was.

While he'd been watching the chaos, Spike hadn't realised he'd continued to tug on his bonds. Sweat and mud stung the cuts he'd now opened on his wrists, but he didn't have time to dwell on it. The diseased rushing him, he glanced over at Hugh. The boy wore a deep scowl and had widened his stance. When the first of the diseased reached him, he jumped up and knocked the thing back with a kick to the face. Mud splashed up where it fell. The beast didn't get up again.

Spike charged the creature closest to him, meeting it rather than waiting for it to attack. He kicked it, driving air and a rancid vinegar tang from its lungs with a boot to the chest.

Where one diseased fell, there were several close behind. Spike could only do so much with his hands bound. As the next creature charged him, he took off, trying to find a route to Hugh across the muddy arena.

Because he had his hands bound, Spike ran like a chicken. The muddy ground threatened to send him flying with every step, but he couldn't worry about it. Deal with it if it happened. He focused on Hugh.

As much as Spike wanted to shout to his friend, Hugh wouldn't hear him over the sounds of the crowd and diseased. It took for them to be within about ten feet of one another for Hugh to look up. He then rushed towards him and they met in the middle. Maybe he understood the plan. Maybe he simply trusted Spike had one.

A few seconds to act, Spike spun around to see three diseased coming for him. Hugh had already knocked two down. Together they kicked them away, two of them falling and one standing back, cautious like an animal that had learned to fear humans.

"Let me untie you," Spike said as he backed towards Hugh.

His eyes on the trepidatious diseased, he fought against his shaking hands to free his friend.

Just as the knot came loose, the diseased charged them again. Hugh stepped in front of Spike and drove a hard fist into the beast's face. The creature howled and fell into the other two, who were only just finding their feet. The crowd cheered.

It gave Hugh time to untie Spike before he took off towards the weapons rack.

Spike ran after his friend and saw the others locked in their own battles with the muzzled diseased. Jamie close by, he ran to the boy, shoved back the two creatures he'd been keeping at bay with his long legs, and quickly untied him.

It gave Jamie the confidence to charge. The diseased overpowered him and took him down.

Spike passed the guards charging to Jamie's aid on his way to the weapons.

Before Spike could reach the rack, Hugh jogged back and handed him what looked to be a replica of Jezebel. He had a broadsword in his other hand.

"Are you sure?" Spike said.

Hugh growled at him. They didn't have time for debate. He attacked the next diseased to rush them, driving the tip of his sword through the centre of its face. The boy fought like Warrior. One hundred percent aggression, he hacked into the already downed creature. No way would it get back up again.

Many of the diseased were still on top of Jamie, giving Spike the chance to look around. Maybe they had the idea on their own, maybe they saw what he and Hugh had just done, but he watched Ranger and Fran untie each other's bonds before they ran towards the weapons rack.

Several diseased on her tail, Fran lost ground to Ranger before she tripped and fell into the mud. Her hands out in front of her as she skidded along, she came to a halt, and three diseased jumped on her back.

Just the three of them left, Ranger made it to the weapons while Spike and Hugh stood back to back and waited for the diseased that were driven their way by the guards.

The axe moved as if it defied gravity. It turned Spike's battle into a dance as he took the muzzled head clean off the first diseased to reach him. The body fell front first into the mud. As another one filled the space behind it, he brought his axe up into the bottom of its chin. It sent the creature falling back, an arc of blood lifting into the air.

The arena damn near shook with the crowd's noise as Spike took two more down, aware of Hugh behind him fighting a similar battle. Then he looked at Ranger; a pack of diseased chased him away from them. Before he could watch the boy for too long, another beast from Jamie's direction charged him, and Spike ended it.

His attention split between the diseased sent their way from the guards and Ranger, the next wave crashed into Spike and Hugh from both sides. Although he tried to swing, a creature from his right collided into him, sending him flying, and he lost his grip on his axe. Sarge's horn sounded before he'd hit the ground. He hadn't given him a chance. He was out.

By the time the guards had cleared the stench of vinegar and rot from him, the hot press of writhing bodies squishing him into the mud, Spike saw about ten of the vile things remained, and Hugh continued to fight them. A pile lay dead at his feet.

Ranger continued to run, several creatures giving chase.

Hugh finished off the ones he'd been fighting and ran after the ones on Ranger's tail. The crowd cheered, clapped, and laughed.

Before Hugh got to them, one of them leaped onto Ranger's back, taking him down to the sound of Sarge's horn.

Hugh stopped as the guards rushed in to gather up the remaining diseased.

The crowd noise rose another level, but instead of taking the praise, Hugh fixed all his attention on Ranger. Caked in blood, the boy from the labs panted like an animal. He'd owned this task. Again. Regardless of Spike's first place in the previous task, if the leaders were to think about selecting the next apprentice at that moment, could Spike really look them in the eyes and make the case it should be him?

CHAPTER 23

They'd worked out until every last drop of daylight the day had to offer had gone—which wasn't a hard thing to accomplish in the depths of winter. Because Spike and Hugh had more training in them, they headed for the gym.

"I hope she's in a better way the next time you see her."

Spike looked at his friend, steam lifting from his sweating head. "Me too. I worry about her so much. I hate how powerless I am to do anything about it."

"You're doing enough."

"Am I? I'm not winning the trials at the moment."

"No, but you're doing your best, and you're still training so you can do better. I have a feeling you'll be okay."

Spike didn't push Hugh for his meaning. Instead, he stared at the gym: light inside, but the curtains drawn. "It's like when we were kids. She'd come into school covered in bruises, and there was nothing I could do about it. We knew what was going on. We all did, even the teachers, but no one intervened. They let her and Artan go home every night to that arsehole."

"It's one of the many prices we pay as a city for national service."

"I'm sorry," Spike said. "Listen to me; I'm sure I'm not the only one who's felt frustrated by the torment and violence brought back into the city from six months outside the wall. Did you ever have it at home?"

While shaking his head, Hugh said, "No. My dad's always been really engaged and emotionally available. Mum's the same."

"We're the lucky ones, eh?"

Hugh looked away as he said, "We sure are."

"At least we're not in Ranger's situation either. He has a dad that's too busy for him, and there's no one else in his life that wants to come and watch him in the trials. No wonder he has the capability to be such a prick."

A few feet from the gym, Spike glanced out over the national service area. He saw the dining hall and the cadets' accommodation beyond. After dark, the cadets were all supposed to be in their dorms—not that they always were though. "Did you know those in the trials were using the gym while we were in our dorms?"

As if unsure whether to take him seriously or not, Hugh watched Spike for a second. "Of course; everyone did."

"Yeah!" Spike laughed. Was he the only one who didn't know? Probably for the best because he would have tried to sneak out to watch them every chance he got. He'd already walked a tightrope to get let into the trials.

Spike reached the gym before Hugh and pulled the door wide, the heat and funk of sweat hitting him as if he'd opened a rancid oven that hadn't fully cooled. As he stepped into the humidity, Hugh behind him, he looked at the lit fire in the corner. It gave off enough light for them to train by, but added to the heat. Just being in the room turned his mouth dry.

The other four stopped what they were doing to watch Spike and Hugh enter. A smile, nothing more, Spike walked to the pile of rocks in the corner.

"We're using them."

Looking at Ranger, Spike saw a slight twitch at the sides of his eyes as if he struggled to keep his emotions in check. Liz, Fran, and Jamie busied themselves with their training. They weren't with the protector's son on this one. Not even Fran.

Two trials in and having not won one yet had certainly challenged Ranger's good nature. His facade had started to slip, flashes of the boy he used to be streaking through him. They didn't need to row though; better to use something else than waste energy on things that didn't matter.

Spike and Hugh moved to the skipping ropes lying on the wooden floor close to the wall covered by the red velvet curtain.

"We're using them too."

His throat even drier for the short amount of time in the gym, Spike filled his lungs and then pressed his lips together to help him hold onto his response. When he looked at Hugh, he saw the same calm expression the boy always wore—too calm now, almost as if he felt nothing.

Spike moved on to the heavy chains that had been salvaged from the ruined city.

"And those."

Of all the people there, Hugh had the right to call the shots, not Ranger. Even though Spike had been trying to avoid the grief, the look on Hugh's face suggested he didn't need to be doing it for his sake. He clearly felt comfortable with the potential confrontation. When he walked back over to the pile of rocks he'd initially gone to, Hugh followed him.

Spike expected Ranger to say something when he lifted one, but the boy managed to keep it in. Hugh lifted the largest rock there.

Ranger didn't go back to working out though; instead, while Liz, Fran, and Jamie continued what they were doing, he said, "They've played to your strengths, you know that?"

Ranger had directed the comment at Hugh, but Hugh said nothing. Instead, he stared straight at the boy, the same calm appraisal in his brown glare.

"I reckon I'll get a few trials that suit me soon. That'll level the playing field."

The lack of Hugh's reply left Ranger's echo to answer him, his face reddening. "What's wrong? You forgotten how to talk, boy?"

At that moment, Fran moved to Ranger's side and placed her hand against his back. Some of his tension left him with the loosening of his shoulders, and he nodded. Yet, when he spoke again, he still delivered it through gritted teeth. "I just want to say well done, Hugh. You've been an excellent competitor so far."

Despite Ranger's change of tack, Hugh's expression remained blank and he continued working out. The atmosphere in the room wound tighter, the only sound coming from Hugh's panting in time with each of his repetitions.

CHAPTER 24

The crunch of cartilage beneath his heavy blows, Hugh clenched his jaw and pounded Ranger's fat head. Punch after punch, he beat his eyes closed, his face bloody and swollen. The boy had so many bruises, he looked like he had rocks beneath his skin, but Hugh didn't stop, hitting his dad's face again and again. That was the last time he'd humiliate him for not being a tailor. The last time …

Hugh stopped and stared down at the mess of a boy. His world blurred, the start of tears burning his eyes. While shaking his head, he lifted the unconscious kid into a sitting position. "James?" More tears streamed down his cheeks. "I'm sorry. I didn't realise it was you. I thought it was—"

Where they'd been swollen shut just seconds previously, James' eyes flew open. His mouth—filled with blood—stretched into a rictus grin. While continuing to smile, Elizabeth's sweet voice formed words with her glistening crimson lips. "Hi, honey."

As Hugh woke, he heard the tail of his startled breath die in the darkness of his room. His heart pounded and he tried to see. While fighting to regulate his breathing, he listened to the deep rhythm of the other three sleeping boys. No matter how many times he blinked, he still saw nothing.

Now he'd woken up, Hugh's need to piss wouldn't let him rest again until he relieved himself. He threw his covers aside, the action waking him up further. Although better to lie awake than to have a night filled with messed-up dreams like the one he'd been experiencing. Dressed just in his underwear, he reached down to the end of his bed to find the trousers and top he'd worn the previous day. They smelled of stale sweat.

Bare feet, Hugh didn't bother looking for his boots. There seemed little point; he'd only be outside for a minute. The cold floorboards questioned his decision, but he pushed on anyway, walking from the room on wobbly legs. Despite his now fully active mind, physical fatigue challenged his ability to remain upright.

At least bare feet made it easier to sneak past the sleeping Sarge in his room. Like with Bleach, the man kept his bedroom door open as if daring the cadets to wake him.

It was late December and it felt like it. Because he only had a T-shirt and trousers on, Hugh's entire body snapped tight as he stepped from their dorm. Would he even be able to piss?

The frosty grass crunched beneath his steps, the ground rock hard as his toes turned numb.

Despite the number of cadets and leaders on the other side of the wall in the national service area, Hugh heard nothing in the still night. The cloudless sky made it colder, but it also turned the moon into a beam, casting silver over everything. Blood. Elizabeth. Lance. Ranger …

Hugh shook his head. It didn't take long for the cycle to start up after he woke, but that didn't stop him hoping today would be the respite he so needed. No such luck.

As the cold worked into his bones, Hugh shook, removing himself from his trousers before he released his bladder against the back wall of their dorm; thankfully it came easily, steam rising from the ground.

Just as Hugh relaxed into the flow, white light smashed against the side of his head. He continued pissing as he fell.

At first just a silhouette, but it didn't take him long to recognise the squat frame looming over him.

Ranger drove a hard kick into Hugh's exposed groin. "You think you're smart, don't you, boy? Well, you're not. You're not smart at all. You're a coward. You're weak."

The second kick slammed into Hugh's right kidney, streaks of the impact running up through his spine. "Come on, boy, fight back."

Hugh stared up at Ranger.

"What's wrong with you?" Ranger leaned down and punched him, sending another explosion of white light through his vision.

As he watched Magma's son, Hugh smiled.

"What are you grinning at?"

Ranger shook while fumbling with his trousers. "I'll give you something to smile about, boy." He removed himself and groaned at the release as he showered Hugh with warm urine.

Hugh remained still while Ranger's hot and stinking piss soaked him.

Once Ranger had finished, Hugh stood up, face-to-face with the boy. Just an inch separated them, Ranger pulling back slightly from what must have been repulsion from the stench of his own waste. It soaked Hugh's hair and dripped from his nose and chin.

While pressing a finger to his temple, Ranger said, "You ain't right in the head, you know that?"

Eyes beaten shut. The twitching limbs of his love. His dad's face. Ranger's smile. Elizabeth's bloody nose.

"Why don't you do something, you coward?"

As much as he might have wanted to, Ranger couldn't hide the tremble in his words. Hugh made a small step forward and

Ranger stepped back. His eyes widened and his voice rose in pitch. "What's wrong with you?"

Hugh smiled and moved another pace forward, forcing Ranger back another step.

"You ain't right." Ranger turned his back on Hugh and walked away from him, muttering, "You ain't right."

Although disconnected from it, Hugh was aware of another smile spreading across his face. Ranger would get his. His time would come. And when it did, it would be glorious.

CHAPTER 25

The sound of Sarge's horn sent the crowd into a frenzy. Spike had learned to hate them already as he stood in the mud, watching Hugh sprint off ahead of him. It must be what it was like to be a protector in the arena. The crowd operated with a strange kind of entitlement. They could treat you however they wanted. They owned you.

Hugh led onto the obstacle course because he had the most points of all the cadets. The rules were simple: keep running the course until you're the only one left. Much like the first task, you were eliminated the second you fell three obstacles behind the leader.

Spike stood in second place. He had Ranger behind him, then Fran, Liz, and Jamie.

The same tree-stump pillars they'd used in the first month of training before they went outside the walls, except the gap between each of them was smaller. They only had to jump half the distance—maybe even less. To watch Hugh climb the first one —the morning frost still on it and mud on his boots from the ground—it made sense. Any farther away and all of them would be out at the first obstacle. They'd be lucky to get through it without breaking bones.

Matilda had flown across the stumps when she'd done it the first time, setting a standard to beat. Hugh's thick frame didn't lend itself to agility, but as he jumped from the first pillar to the next, Spike looked at Sarge. The man gave him the nod to go.

Up on the first pillar, Spike's mind flashed back to the ruined city, to when he saw Matilda on the plinth, surrounded by diseased desperate to end her. He looked for her in the crowd.

"Come on!" Ranger screamed.

Hugh had crossed three stumps already. A shake of his head, Spike used Matilda's method, jumping from one to the next until he landed with a squelch directly behind his friend.

Two ropes hung down from a platform about twenty feet up. They had knots tied into them at regular intervals. The cold had worked into Spike's knuckles, challenging his grip, but he still moved up quicker than Hugh, overtaking him to reach the platform first.

At the other side of the platform, Spike came to a large net that led to the ground. He jumped on it, his stomach lurching when it sagged more than he'd expected, but he held on, spun around, and climbed backwards to the bottom.

A ten-foot wall next, Spike charged at it, the muddy ground sapping his forward momentum. He leaped, kicked off against the wooden barrier, and grabbed the top. He pulled himself over, flinging his legs so he landed on the other side. Instead of the squelch he expected, he came down with a thud and looked at his feet to see the wooden sheet covering the pit. The noise of the crowd was damn near deafening, but he could have sworn he felt the banging of fists through the soles of his boots.

Next, Spike came to a cargo net stretched across the ground. He dived beneath it and looked over to see Jamie moving along the tops of the tall pillars. The hard rope hurt his head, but he dropped his focus and butted his way through to the other side. As he stood up—breathing hard—Sarge's horn sounded, halting Jamie just before he leaped from the final log.

Before Spike could run back to the stumps, he saw a guard waving him in a different direction. He followed his instruction, locking into a rhythm with his breathing and steps, heading for the arena's exit. Silly him for thinking the assault course would be so straightforward.

Outside the arena, Spike saw another guard who waved him over. His legs were already on fire. Had he given too much too soon? Any doubt he'd had trebled when he saw where the guard pointed. The tunnel Ranger had goaded him about when they were training during the first month of national service. The tunnel he'd told him had diseased in it. The tunnel he'd had a panic attack in front of and never managed to enter. An instant tightening of his chest, he slowed down and shook his head. He couldn't do it. He couldn't.

Spike glanced over his shoulder to see Hugh and then Ranger emerging from the arena. It was just a tunnel. There were no diseased in it before, so why would there be now?

Hugh caught up to Spike, but instead of running past him, he grabbed a handful of the back of his shirt and threw him forward so he landed on all fours at the tunnel's entrance. The rich reek of damp earth overwhelmed him as he listened for the sounds of diseased inside. Hugh didn't let up, shoving him forward again so he shot head first into the tunnel.

Spike crawled forwards, Hugh pushing him from behind. His chest tightened and stars flashed through his vision. Cramps threatened to lock his limbs and he shook his head. Yet as much as he wanted to stop, Hugh wouldn't let him, shoving him every time he slowed down.

Then Ranger entered the tunnel. "Come on, Spike, get a move on, you pussy."

Something changed in Spike. The voice of his once tormentor reminded him how far he'd come. A dark tunnel had nothing on what he'd experienced. As his chest unwound, Spike's limbs loosened and he quickened his pace. Where he expected another shove from Hugh, it didn't come. He didn't need it.

Seeing daylight up ahead, Spike used it as his goal.

The cold winter air hit Spike like fresh water against his face as he burst free. He jumped to his feet and sprinted back into the arena, the crowd regaining their voice as he headed for the wooden pillars, where Liz now stood with Jamie because she'd been eliminated too, but Sarge redirected him, sending him under the cargo net to go back through the course the other way.

Out of the cargo net, Spike threw himself over the wall and finally saw Hugh with Ranger and Fran behind him. They should have been closer. Had Hugh held them all up in the tunnel?

The squelch of the muddy ground beneath his steps, Spike sprinted for the net leading up to the platform with the ropes hanging from it. The wide obstacle swung as he climbed, fatigue robbing some of his strength. The swaying momentum threatened to eat away at his progress.

When Spike reached the platform, he dropped to his knees, backed off the ledge, and caught the rope with his dangling feet. He shook as sweat stung his eyes. He started his descent while Hugh climbed out of the cargo net, Ranger and Fran still behind him.

The friction from the coarse rope bit into Spike's hands, his grip still weak from the cold. For the final few feet, his climb turned into a fall, his legs failing him when he landed. The cold mud soaked through the seat of his trousers.

His palms on fire from the rope burns, Spike ran for the wooden pillars, climbed up onto the first one, and leaped from one side to the other. When his feet sank into the mud at the other end, Sarge sounded his horn. Fran was out.

Another lap, Spike ran outside the arena. If he had any chance of winning this, he couldn't rely on Hugh to shove him into the tunnel again. He had to be brave.

Like with the rest of the course, the guards showed Spike he now needed to go through the tunnel the other way. Something about it helped. A different experience to the one he'd had when he'd panicked, he dived into the tunnel, shifting through it on all fours and emerging from the other side before sprinting back to the arena.

On his way back, Spike passed Hugh, who smiled and winked at him. He reached the wooden pillars, which Ranger was still crossing. The red-faced boy looked like he wanted to swing for him as he finally jumped from the last one.

The same method he'd used every time, Spike flew across the top of the pillars. A lizard crossing a hot desert, the pat of his feet against the poles ended with another resounding squelch as he landed.

Lactic acid bit into Spike's biceps while he ascended the rope, his body shaking, his chest tight. Relying on his legs, he pushed off against every knot, scrambling up onto the platform before rolling off onto the cargo net.

The same ten-foot wall, Spike stretched his mouth wider to help him breathe as he charged, the cold air burning his lungs. He leaped at the wooden wall, kicked off it, caught the top, and threw himself over.

Fatigue made Spike clumsy, and he snagged his leg on the top. If anything, it increased his momentum, throwing him to the ground. He landed on his back against the wooden cover, the impact driving the wind from his lungs.

As he lay there, gasping for breath—the diseased beneath him banging against the hatch of their wooden prison—Spike heard Sarge blow two loud toots. He let go of his need to get to his feet and smiled. He'd done it!

CHAPTER 26

Every step sent a streak up Spike's back—the pain from the fall on the wooden sheet still with him—but as he walked to the gym and beyond the cloying mud of the arena, his movements grew easier. The winner of the third trial, he now shared the lead with Hugh with thirteen points and was three ahead of Ranger in third.

Spike followed the other cadets towards the large wooden structure, squinting against the bright and low sun when he looked up at the tall roof he and Matilda had climbed on while on national service. Sure, he'd been fighting to stay alive then, and fighting for the approval of his team leaders, which proved a trickier task, but at least he knew what they required of him. His head had been a mess during the trials. Of course, he had to win, but he had no idea how to manage Ranger and his current attempt at charm, nor Hugh, who was there one minute and away with the fairies the next. No matter how often he tried to get his friend to open up, the boy shut him down.

Fran and Jamie entered the gym behind Ranger and Liz. Spike followed after Hugh. The place smelled of damp from being mopped earlier that day. Damp and sweat. No matter how many times they cleaned it, they couldn't remove the reek of exercise. Because no one else stopped to clean their boots at the door, he didn't either, dragging mud from the arena into the clean hut.

Spike jumped when Matilda rushed at him and wrapped him in a tight hug. While wincing against the pain in his back, he forced his words out with his gasp. "You seem better."

Whenever Matilda felt embarrassed, her cheeks glowed like they were glowing now. She'd clearly forgotten herself for a moment, moving back a step to give Spike and his dad a chance to embrace.

Before Spike asked Matilda what had happened, he led her and his dad to a corner. No chance of privacy in the open space, but they didn't have to stand in the centre of the room either.

As they walked in silence, Spike took in the room. Hugh stood in one corner with his brother and mum, the other cadets with people close to them. Then he saw Ranger. The short and squat boy surveyed the gym from beneath a thick and furrowed brow. From how his gaze roved, it looked like he didn't know where to let it settle. His cheeks were flushed red, and it looked like his eyes watered as he shifted from one foot to the other. Almost as if the motion would allow him to squirm free from his discomfort.

Before Spike could ask Matilda what had happened, Ranger's childish whine went off in the large wooden room. "I don't know why I'm here. You already know my dad's busy outside the wall. Why make me go through this *every time*?" He spoke the last of it through gritted teeth.

Silence fell on the place, and many of the people there looked anywhere but at Ranger.

His rage directed at Sarge by the door, Ranger shrugged. "Well?"

In what looked like a clear attempt to avoid the drama, Sarge crossed the gym to get to Ranger. It only served to heighten it, his loud and awkward gait hitting the wooden floor with a metronomic thud. With every step, Spike felt his shoulders tighten, the bruising in his lower back twinging from the involuntary reaction.

Sarge put an arm around Ranger. For a second, it seemed like the boy might resist. Then he glanced at those in the room. They'd initially been afraid to look back, but now they stared straight at him. Still as red-faced as before, he let Sarge lead him from the gym.

Like everyone else there, Spike braced when winter rushed in through the open door, and he waited for it to close before returning his attention to Matilda and his dad.

Although Matilda looked ready to burst with what she had to tell him, Spike's dad stepped forward first and hugged him again. "I think Matilda needs you today. Well done on your win, and I'll be here next month, okay?"

Despite being taller than the man, Spike always felt safe in his dad's strong arms and held on for a second longer than he needed to. As he watched his dad walk away, he smiled.

"So," Matilda said the second he turned around, "Jan has stopped being a bitch."

"That's good—"

"There's more."

"I assumed, what's going on?"

Her hands clasped together in front of her, Matilda bounced on the spot, her face alive for the first time since Artan's incarceration. "She saw *everything*."

Spike waited.

"What happened with Mum and Dad. How Artan acted in self-defence."

"And she's prepared to give a statement?"

Matilda nodded so rapidly Spike could have sworn he heard her rattle. "That's amazing!"

"I *know*." Tears filled her eyes, the firelight rippling on the saline layer. "I think we're going to get Artan out."

CHAPTER 27

For the week or so before the trials and for a few days after, they locked the arena for set-up and take down, so Spike and Hugh had to train with the others in the gym. With every task, they'd locked the gates for longer. The trial with the tunnel only yesterday, how long would it be before they let them back in this time?

Still early enough for the grass to be frozen from the cold night, Spike dug his hands deep in his pockets, his neck pulled into his shoulders as he walked beside Hugh. "So by the time this is over, Artan might be out."

"That's amazing," Hugh said.

"I know, right? But now it's on me to make sure I win this thing."

"I don't think you need to worry about that. Just keep doing what you're doing."

Maybe it was Spike's pride that stopped him asking Hugh if he'd held Ranger up in the tunnel on the previous task. Maybe he didn't care. After all, he accepted he'd been handed first place when he knew Hugh could have beaten him. He'd trained with him enough to see a different boy had returned from his month away. More capable, sure, but the biggest change had happened between his ears. The boy no longer had an off switch. Where he would have given up before attempting a task, he didn't seem to even consider it now. He could push himself as far as he needed to. Further than any of the other cadets in the trials. Despite several attempts to get him to talk about how he felt and what had gone on in the month away, Hugh remained hostile to any questioning.

"How's your back?" Hugh said.

"Better. Sleep and rest have helped. I think I'll be able to run it off."

At the door to the gym, Spike opened it and walked into the still-cold room first, breaking through his own clouds of condensation as he expelled them. The same smell of wood he always picked up on when he entered the place hung in the air. Although the others were there, they didn't appear to have started exercising.

As Spike and Hugh walked over to the large rocks they used as weights, Ranger said, "We're using them."

Spike didn't look at the boy and then saw Hugh didn't either.

"I said *we're using them.*"

Where Spike would have expected Hugh to warm up first, he watched his friend go straight for the largest rock and lift it while glaring at Ranger.

The tension in the room tightened, Hugh's thick arms bulging with his reps. If Ranger walking over bothered him, he didn't show it, staring at Magma's son while he continued to bicep curl the large weight.

"So, first you hold me up in the tunnel, and now you want to get in the way of my training? Do you really feel that threatened by me?"

The only response Hugh gave came in the form of hard breathing from the effort of lifting the rock.

Ranger looked across at Jamie, Fran, and Liz. Bouncing as if he wanted to let loose on Hugh, he shook his head. "I get it. You want to play games with me, yeah? Well, if that's the case, how about we play a little game? Or, if you'd rather, I can keep kicking your arse?"

Spike snorted a laugh.

"Something funny, boy?"

"Ain't no way you're kicking his arse. No way."

All the while, Hugh stared straight at Ranger and lifted his rock.

"Did he tell you I kicked him to the ground and pissed on him the other night?"

Spike looked at Hugh. Hugh remained fixed on Ranger.

"That he lay there like a wounded animal while I emptied my bladder all over him? I even let him get to his feet. When he did, he still didn't have the minerals to react."

Another rep followed by another rep. Hugh still didn't bite from Ranger's provocation.

"Come on, Hugh, admit you held me up in the tunnel on the last trial. No way should I have gone out when I did. If you'd have gotten out of my way and not helped your liability of a mate, I would have won the last one."

In the face of Ranger's accusation, Spike tensed, but he followed Hugh's lead and kept his mouth shut. Arguing with Ranger rarely led to anything positive.

"So how about it? A little game to test who's the best competitor. *Without* cheating."

Liz stepped forward, "Do we really need to do this? We're already competing against one another."

The room ignored her, and Hugh ignored Ranger, lowering the large rock to the gym's wooden floor.

"So? You've hit me where it hurts. You've given your boy the points, so just indulge me in a little game, yeah?"

While throwing his arm in the direction of the others, Ranger said, "They're up for it. It's a bit of fun. A way to release the tension."

"*I'm* not up for it," Liz said.

The room ignored her for a second time.

Hugh turned his back on Ranger and looked at Spike. "What do you think?"

It sounded insane, but maybe Ranger needed to be put in his place yet again. His back still sore from his fall in the ring, but not so bad he couldn't train, Spike shrugged. "Sure. Why not?"

Spike joined the line stretching across one end of the gym, Hugh on one side of him, Fran, Jamie, and Liz on the other. Ranger stood in the middle of the room, a wide smile to go with his sadistic glare. "It's quite a simple game, really. It's one we used to play as kids. It's called *diseased*."

All his senses on high alert, Spike glanced at the red curtain running down the wall on his right. Did Ranger have something behind there? Did he plan on letting something out on them?

"*I'm* the diseased."

If Fran and Jamie were in on Ranger's plan to play a game, they certainly didn't give off that impression. Frowns and sideways glances, if Spike opted out, would they join him? Liz would for sure. Although, Hugh looked up for it, staring straight at Ranger.

"I'll stand in the middle here," Ranger said, "and you have to get past me. That's it. Simple." For the next few seconds, Ranger and Hugh locked eyes. "And don't worry, Hugh, I'll go easy on you. Okay. Are you all ready?"

No one replied, and for a second time Spike considered leading a walkout, but something kept him there. What had gone on between Hugh and Ranger when no one else was around? How would this play out?

Ranger's voice exploded through the large hall. "Go!"

Spike joined Fran, Jamie, and Liz in jogging to the other side. All the while, Ranger stared at Hugh, letting them all past.

"I said *go*."

His fists balled, his head dipped so he led with his brow, Hugh broke into a jog towards Ranger. That was when Spike saw it: the glint of a blade down the back of Ranger's trousers. It wasn't the first time he'd done it, so how did he not realise what was going on sooner? Of course Ranger would stoop that low, but it all happened too quickly for him to do anything other than call out, "Hugh!"

The early morning sunlight shone in through the gym's windows, lighting up the long blade as Ranger drew it.

If Hugh felt intimidated by the weapon, he didn't show it, bringing his hand around in one fluid movement and chopping Ranger's wrist. The long knife spun as it skittered across the gym's wooden floor. In the moment where Ranger watched it, Hugh could have blindsided him, dropped him with one bang. Instead, he stopped directly in front of him and waited. He wouldn't give the boy any excuses.

Ranger yelled and punched Hugh in the face. The loud crack sent a wince through Spike, and he nearly went to his friend's aid. Hugh clearly didn't need it though; other than his head snapping from the attack, the boy barely moved.

As Ranger swung at him again, Hugh blocked it, parrying his blow with his left forearm. He still said nothing, moving close enough to Ranger so their noses nearly touched. The sound of Ranger's gasps filled the large hall, and he cowered in the face of Hugh's might.

Hugh shoved the boy aside with enough force to throw him to the floor. He then joined the other cadets.

Still gasping, Ranger jumped to his feet, and Spike tensed to watch him run for the knife. But when he'd retrieved it, instead of charging Hugh, he bolted from the gym.

Spike broke the silence. "Wow! What happened there?"

Liz snorted. "I dunno, but I can almost taste the testosterone."

A second later, Fran left the building, a cold rush of air sweeping in before the door fell shut again.

CHAPTER 28

The shaking bed woke Spike, and he instinctively clung to the side of it to prevent himself from falling out. While fighting against his rapid pulse, he found his bearings in time to make out the silhouette leaving the room. Too dark to be one hundred percent sure, but it looked like Hugh.

The rhythmic sound of deep respiration told Spike that Ranger and Jamie were still asleep. While holding his breath as if it would help him move with more stealth—as if it would stop the bed creaking in response to his shifting weight—he slowly climbed down to the wooden floor.

Spike jumped the final foot and landed with a heavier thud than he'd anticipated. His semi-naked body tensed from the cold, but before finding his clothes, he listened to Ranger and Jamie again. They continued to breathe deeply. Still unable to see much, he had to trust his ears.

After he'd thrown on yesterday's clothes, Spike walked on tiptoes to his boots by the door. He slipped them on before running out into the cold night in time to see Hugh jogging into the arena. It had been closed earlier that day, so they must have only just reopened it. How soon would they close it again so they could set up for the fourth trial? Would it remain shut all month for the fifth one? No doubt they had torture of unparalleled horror planned for the cadets for their finale, something to send them off with a bang.

It took a few steps for Spike's tired legs to find their stride, but he managed to get into a rhythm, the frigid air burning his eyes and lungs simultaneously. He jogged into the arena's entrance, his heavy steps and hard breaths accentuated by the tighter space.

Hugh jumped from the darkness with his fists raised.

Spike let out a nervous laugh while backing off and holding his hands up as if he'd just been told to freeze. "Why didn't I see that kind of fight earlier today?"

"What the hell are you talking about?"

They continued into the arena, walking the perimeter of the ring. Spike looked at the empty seats. It could have been a different place compared to the one they entered on trial days. "With Ranger. What was that earlier?"

"I'm guessing he feels insecure about me beating him."

"Duh!"

"Well, why ask me, then?"

"What I mean is, what was going on with you? You could have put Ranger in his place ten times over in the gym earlier. Why didn't you? And did he really piss on you?"

"It's not worth it. You know what he's like. He's a rat. The second I lay a finger on him, he'll give Daddy the evidence he needs to get me kicked off the trials. I'm much better keeping my head down and beating him in here. No one can take it away from me then."

The moon emerged from behind a dark cloud, the frosty ground glistening beneath its glow. When Spike looked at his friend, Hugh refused to look back. The fact that he hadn't denied being pissed on … "What's going on with you? Ranger's been going for you since day one, hasn't he?"

Hugh stared ahead with a hard frown.

"You're not the Hugh I used to know. I want to help you, but if you won't talk to me, I'm not sure there's anything I can do."

"Who said I need help?" The end of his sentence echoed through the large arena.

Maybe he had a point. Where did Spike get off telling Hugh he needed to talk?

"You sound like my brother and mum. They always want to talk things out. But my dad has a theory about talking. He says it's for pussies. That it doesn't matter how you feel because Edin doesn't give a shit."

"And you think that's the way to be, do you? Besides, *I* give a shit."

"We have to suck it up and get on with it. Take all our hurt and pain and stuff it down, because no matter how much we talk, it doesn't take away the memories. It doesn't stop the hurt." His voice faltered when he said, "It won't resurrect Elizabeth."

To study Hugh's face in the newly present moonlight showed Spike the start of tears in his eyes. "But it might ease your pain a little, even if it's just by the smallest amount. You need to let it in by taking one small step at a time."

Hugh stopped dead, and Spike expected him to turn his way. Instead, he stared into the centre of the arena and raised a shaking hand while pointing across the space.

When Spike saw why he'd halted, his stomach tightened and the hairs on the back of his neck stood on end.

"What the …? Maybe it fell off in the last task?" The echo of his hopeful words came back at him from the walled ring as if mocking his suggestion.

Hugh ran towards the centre of the arena.

By the time Spike caught up, Hugh had stopped by the

wooden hatch covering the pit. He held the muzzle he'd just picked up from the frozen ground.

The light might have been limited, but not so limited Spike didn't see what Hugh showed him. "It's been cut."

"And I can take a good guess at who did it."

"You really think he'd let out a diseased?" Spike said.

"Absolutely."

"Shit. Do you think it was intended for you?"

"Definitely. Maybe both of us."

Spike and Hugh ran for the arena's exit. Side by side, Spike's feet twisted and turned over the unyielding frozen ground.

Hugh emerged first and Spike a second later. They both halted and stared back at their dorm. Sarge, Ranger, Fran, and Liz all stood outside. Liz kneeled down, holding her face with both hands. Her sobs carried through the still night. Two inanimate bodies lay in front of her. One of them had a sword protruding from their head from where it had been pinned to the ground.

"Dammit," Hugh said. "We're too late."

CHAPTER 29

As Spike and Hugh walked closer to the dorm, Liz released a deep braying sound before she fell back into heavy sobs. Every impulse challenged Spike's forward momentum. "I don't understand," he said. "Why didn't we pass him on the way in?" As much as he didn't want to look, his eyes rested on the body pinned to the ground: what had once been Jamie. The body next to it must have been the owner of the muzzle.

"I'm guessing Ranger saw us coming and managed to hide. It's dark enough. I—"

Spike waited for a second for Hugh to continue, and when he didn't, he turned to see Sarge marching over. Still twenty feet between them, he jabbed an accusatory finger their way. "Where have you two been?"

When Hugh didn't speak, Spike remained mute too, his attention moving to Ranger by the dorm. The boy stared straight back, not a hint of guilt in his dark eyes.

"Well?"

Sarge's voice dragged Spike's attention from Ranger back to their team leader. Spike then took the muzzle from Hugh and held it out in a shaking hand. "We found this in the arena." He held it up to the light. "It looks like someone cut it from the face of a diseased."

A look from Spike to Hugh, and Sarge said, "Well, there are two quite obvious culprits standing in front of me."

"Why would *we* set a diseased loose on the dorm?"

"You tell me. And then you can explain it to Jamie's family. It was bad enough having to kill the kid; now I need to go through what happened with those who loved him."

The way Sarge used past tense hit Spike like a gut punch. The cold combined with his adrenaline sent a furious shake through him. His words warbled and his eyes watered as fire rose through his body. It took all he had to refrain from shouting. "It makes no sense. Hugh and I are in first and second place in the trials. None of the other cadets are a threat to us."

"Maybe you did it as a prank gone wrong?"

"Not very funny though, is it?"

"Watch your mouth, boy."

Spike balled his fists as a way to spend some of the energy coursing through him. "With all due respect, Sarge, you're accusing Hugh and me of murder. I have *every* right to defend that ludicrous assertion."

The tension between the two tightened, Spike damn near cramping up because of it. As if challenged by Spike's rage, Sarge stepped so close Spike felt his body heat.

Another glance at Ranger, the boy stared back with his usual compassionless glare. What did Spike expect? An admission of guilt?

While rubbing his temples and letting out a hard exhale, his hot breath smothering Spike, Sarge said, "I didn't see who did this."

"Then you weren't watching Ranger closely enough," Spike said.

"You need to know when to keep your mouth shut."

"Just making an observation, *sir*. And with my back against the wall like it currently is, I feel like I have to defend myself."

"You're walking on the edge, boy. I suggest you wind your neck in, keep your head down, and get on with the trials. We're already one cadet down; we can't afford to lose any more without the crowd rioting. Were it not for that, you'd be out already."

It helped Spike keep quiet, and he bit down on his bottom lip as if to hold on to his reaction.

"Like I said, I didn't see who did this, but I *will* find out. Until then, we carry on. You hear me?"

Spike shook with adrenaline and cold. Despite wanting to say so much more, he acknowledged Sarge with a nod before walking towards his dorm to the sound of Liz's crying.

CHAPTER 30

It had been close to a month since Jamie's death, and although no one had spoken about it since, Liz, of all the cadets, hadn't been the same and was now prone to moments of inconsolable grief. Spike hadn't realised how much she'd cared for the boy because he and Hugh had distanced themselves as much as they could. Jamie's passing had divided the group, the cadets picking sides based on their assumptions. Fran and Liz now spent all their time with Ranger, and Spike spent all his with Hugh. Sarge had even agreed to let Ranger sleep in the girls' room to save any more drama. Other than the assumption from Liz, Sarge, and possibly Fran that Spike and Hugh played some part in releasing the diseased, it suited everyone just fine. They were now two separate camps, competing against one another in the ring, and strangers when they passed in the hallways or trained in the gym.

Despite Spike's previous experiences, he still hadn't gotten used to standing in the arena, the attention of the crowd on him and the other cadets. Because his dad and Matilda sat in roughly the same area, it only took him a few seconds to locate them this time around. Hard to tell from the distance between them, but Matilda still looked well. She had her hair tied up and sat with a straight posture. He hoped she'd progressed with her case to free Artan. His dad smiled and gave him a thumbs up.

For the past few minutes, Spike had stood in a line with the other competitors. Hugh on his right, Ranger, Fran, and Liz on his left. Each of them stared down a long corridor. Six tall wooden walls created five long and straight tunnels running almost the entire width of the arena. The walls stretched away from them as long panels at least twenty feet tall and were placed so close to one another the tunnels were no more than three feet wide.

The noise of the crowd died down, Spike craning his neck to see the reason for it as Sarge walked into view. The same grizzled look he always wore, had Spike not witnessed firsthand just how miserable the man was, he would have sworn he did it for effect. He walked with his usual hobble, his loud hailer gripped in his right hand. Were he a more affable man, a cadet might have asked him where he picked up the injury; but the less you asked Sarge, the better.

Sarge lifted the metal cone to his mouth and shouted, "Ladies and gentlemen, boys and girls, we've made it really simple today. All the cadets have to do is get from here to the other end of their corridor. The first one out is the winner."

Although Spike stood in the same stunned silence as the cadets on either side of him and many of the crowd directly behind, the crowd on the other side of the arena laughed and clapped. A glance at Hugh, Spike shrugged. Who knew what they had planned.

A guard then appeared with five broadswords in her arms. She walked down the line of cadets, handing them out, starting with Hugh. After he'd pinched the screws and twisted them to check their tightness, Hugh swapped swords with Spike and did the same with his weapon.

Sarge raised the metal cone to his mouth again. "There are no rules in this trial. Anything goes."

The statement clearly excited Ranger, whose mouth stretched into a wide grin, and his dark eyes darkened.

The crowd at the other end of the tunnels continued to laugh, whipping themselves into a frenzy.

"On my count, you need to get to the other end of the corridor as quickly as you can. Three ... two ..."

Maybe if Spike had given it more thought, he would have seen it coming. No thought needed now as the shriek from the diseased lifted the hairs on the back of his neck. It sent a cold chill running through him, and he barely heard Sarge's horn, his focus purely on the swarm of what must have been at least twenty muzzled creatures in his corridor.

The creatures had nowhere to run but forward, adrenaline surging through Spike as he watched the guards shut a gate across the end of his corridor. Hugh had already charged into action.

A flash of light then smashed into Spike from his left. His world spun, his ears rang, and for a moment, his legs nearly buckled beneath him. Before he'd gathered his bearings to retaliate against Ranger's attack, the boy grabbed Spike's sword from him and threw it into the alley. The large weapon landed in the mud between him and the diseased.

Although the crowd behind them booed, Ranger kicked Spike in the backside, shouting, "You'd best retrieve your weapon, boy."

Spike stumbled forward, tripped, and crashed down to his knees in the muddy ground at the mouth of the corridor. He could deal with Ranger later. What currently mattered rushed towards him as a frenzied, snapping, and foetid mess.

CHAPTER 31

I t didn't matter that most of the crowd had witnessed it; Sarge had said there were no rules. His hands and knees covered in mud, no more than fifty feet separated Spike and the diseased rushing towards him. The close press of the wooden walls on either side heightened their vinegar reek. The creatures were yet to reach his sword, but Ranger had thrown it too far for him to get to it first.

A ringing in his ears and half of his face numb from where Ranger had sucker-punched him, Spike stood up to face the onrushing fury forty feet away.

Even in his tunnel, he had a view of Matilda. To see her face gave him the answer he needed.

Spike removed one of his boots and threw it at the first diseased with all he had. It hit the creature square in the face. The shock of it slowed the beast down for a few steps. He removed his second boot before throwing that one too. The boos behind him turned into laughter. They might think he'd lost his mind, but he had a plan.

His socks as sodden as his hands and knees, Spike ripped one and then the other off, discarding them both.

Twenty feet.

Spike jumped into the air and made a star with his limbs, pressing against the flat wooden walls on either side with his bare hands and feet. While pushing hard with his hands, he pulled his feet up. He then pressed hard with his feet. The pressure drove the white-hot pain of splinters into his exposed soles and palms, but he clenched his jaw through it and reached higher with his hands.

Just as Spike pulled his feet up for a second time, the lead diseased caught up to him and swung wildly in his direction. It missed dragging him to the ground by only a few inches. Had it reached him a second sooner … he shuddered to think about it, the creatures' stench worse than ever.

When he'd climbed about ten feet up, Spike levelled his breathing while fighting against his shaking hands and legs. After a moment to compose himself, he kept a tight press on first his hands and then his feet as he made his way down the corridor. The crowd on both sides cheered his name. A moment to look at Matilda, he saw she and his dad had joined in with the chants.

Picking up momentum, Spike found his rhythm. He passed over his broadsword, the weapon caked in mud from where it had been trampled. A small gap in the diseased, the thought to retrieve it crossed his mind, but with just over half the corridor to go, he'd get there quicker if he avoided the fight.

Pressure on his feet, then hands, then feet, Spike picked up his momentum, scooting over the heads of the furious creatures crammed into the space below. They all stared up at him through crimson eyes, their movements twitchy, their mouths snapping as a useless gesture. To look at them made him think about what Ranger had done to Jamie, and it derailed his concentration. He thought about the now silent accusations levelled at him and Hugh. He shook his head to clear it; in that moment, it served no purpose.

It took a few minutes, but Spike made it, swinging from the

corridor, clearing the gate at the end, and landing with a squelch on the other side. The cold mud squeezed up through his toes, reassuring him of his now solid footing. When he found Matilda in the crowd again, she nodded and smiled.

Maybe he should have looked at his fellow competitors first because he only just saw that Ranger and Hugh had beaten him to the end. Hugh wore the diseased's blood like a second skin, feral in how he panted, his eyes wide, his thick frame hunched. Hugh looked how he expected him to; Ranger, on the other hand, had emerged from his corridor spotless.

As Spike opened his mouth to question it, the volume of the crowd lifted, Liz falling over the gate at the end of her corridor as she crossed the finish line. Like Hugh, she wore the diseased's blood. Sarge's horn then sounded. Fran had clearly failed.

The crowd quieted down when Sarge appeared. "Well—" he laughed "—I did say there weren't any rules other than to get to the end of your corridor first. And, Ranger, you got there first. Not that I condone you punching William, but this wasn't a test of morals."

"Luckily for him," Spike said, the crowd noise dropping in response.

"As things stand, we're going into the last trial with Hugh in the lead, William in second, and Ranger in third. We've decided to give the winner of the next trial a bonus of five points. To save complicating things, whoever wins the final trial wins the apprenticeship outright."

Spike watched the grinning Ranger, who winked at him. "Looks like it's all to play for, loser."

With everything in the balance, Spike had the wherewithal to hold onto his reply. They had one trial left, and now all he had to do was come first. He had to live up to his part of the deal and let the leaders decide the rest, but he still didn't understand how Ranger had remained immaculate.

As if he'd heard Spike's silent question, Hugh came close and said, "He ran around the outside rather than down his corridor."

"Cheating bastard."

"Sarge doesn't agree. And now we have the contrived crowd-pleasing drama of it all coming down to the final trial."

CHAPTER 32

At least they'd got the message that Ranger didn't want to go to the gym after the trials. It had grown increasingly awkward for everyone involved to see the boy stand on his own, red-faced and glowering at anyone who dared look at him.

"It's a good job they kept that little rat away," Spike's dad said, loud enough for everyone else to hear. "Cheating little shit!"

"I don't think we should be having this conversation," Matilda said, looking at the other friends and family in the room. "Besides, Ranger wants Spike to get mad. It's the only way he can beat him."

It helped Spike relax a little. "Thank you," he said.

"The apprenticeship is there for the taking. Win the next trial and it's yours. Maybe Ranger's played his hand too early; you now know what he's prepared to do to win."

No matter how Spike tried to focus on the actions he needed to take, he couldn't ignore the nagging thought that had eaten away at him for the past few weeks. What if Hugh beat him? He gained nothing from thinking about it; it didn't change that he needed to win. Best to focus on his performance and then deal with the outcome. Before his thoughts overwhelmed him, he turned to his dad. "How's Mum?"

A dark scowl from where he clearly couldn't let go of what had happened in the arena, Spike's dad shrugged. "She's Mum, you know how she gets."

"Can you tell her I love her?"

"Will do."

"And, Tilly? What's going on with Artan?"

"Jan and I are putting a case together. We're just waiting to meet with a politician."

"It all sounds hopeful."

To see Matilda smile pushed away some of the dark cloud over Spike's head. "Yeah, we're planning to have him out before you come home. So you don't need to worry about us, okay? Just make sure you win this thing."

One of the guards stepped away from the wall and cleared his throat. "Right, ladies and gentlemen, visiting's over."

After another hug with his dad, Spike held onto Matilda. "Love you."

She kissed his neck, her warm breath tickling his ear as she leaned closer. "You too. Now win this for both of us. I have every faith in you."

His mood well and truly lifted, Spike smiled for what felt like the first time in weeks as he watched his love and his dad leave the gym. He had this. His destiny would be decided by his own actions.

CHAPTER 33

Hugh ran like he always did. A simple action, he needed to focus on putting one foot in front of the other, and if he pushed himself hard enough, it stopped him thinking about anything else. His breaths visible, the sun barely risen, he ran around the perimeter of the arena in the grainy light, the frosty grass yielding to his every step as his feet sank into the soft mud beneath.

As Hugh found his squelching rhythm, his mind wandered. Elizabeth. Her bloody nose. Ranger so close to him for so long during their time at the trials, and he'd done nothing. In fact, he'd let him behave worse. Lance's face. The boy in woodwork. He quickened his pace, his lungs burning from the cold air, his legs sore. Every muscle in his body ached. Rest days were supposed to be important for conditioning, but Hugh took none because rest days opened the door for the demons. Running kept him patient. He had a plan, and if he intended to follow it, he needed to keep his head.

It had snowed a few weeks previously, the thawing of it turning the ground even muddier. It clung to Hugh's every step, dragging on his momentum and sapping the energy from his already fatigued muscles.

As Hugh came around the back side of the large arena for the third time, their dorm came into view again. Every time he saw the dorm, he went closer to the wooden hut in case Spike had woken up and was waiting for him.

Hugh's chest tightened to see not only Spike standing outside, but Ranger just a foot in front of him. Whatever they were talking about, they both had their chests puffed out and their fists balled.

Counter to every urge coursing through him, Hugh slowed down. In his mind, he charged Ranger, knocked him to the ground, and kicked him unconscious. Kicked him dead. In his mind, he'd already done it a thousand times. The blood. Elizabeth's twitching limbs. Lance's swollen face. That wouldn't get him anywhere though; besides, Spike might not want his help.

Spike and Ranger were so locked in their conversation they hadn't noticed Hugh's approach. When Ranger stepped towards Spike, Hugh moved closer so he could hear what they said to one another.

"You cheated, you snake," Spike said. "I would have beaten you on the last trial had you not done that to my sword."

"No, you would have charged down your tunnel like Hugh did, but you would have been slower than him and still come third. At least by throwing your sword I gave you an opportunity to show off to the crowd. Me winning the last trial came from being able to see the bigger picture."

"Was letting the diseased out of the pit to kill Jamie seeing the bigger picture? Surely if you'd have seen the bigger picture, you would have realised Hugh and I weren't in the dorm. I mean, we were your targets, right?"

Despite recovering his breath, Hugh's heart quickened when the short Ranger shook his head. What he'd give to take a brick to the back of his skull. His body wound even tighter when Ranger said, "I *didn't* let that diseased out. You and your strange little friend did."

Images of blood crashed into Hugh's mind, surging to the fore as Spike shoved Ranger away from him. As much as he wanted to rush to his friend's side, he wouldn't stop if he attacked Ranger now. He needed to wait. Although, what he needed to do and what he did were two different things. Hugh ran at the pair.

Just before Spike swung for Ranger, Hugh stepped between them, his back to Magma's son as he held his hands up, imploring Spike. "Don't!"

"Get out of the way, Hugh."

Now he had someone between him and Spike, Ranger grew in confidence. Like every coward who loved the bravado more than the fight, he grew deadlier as the chances of an actual brawl dwindled. Hugh could have sworn he heard him say 'let me at him'. But he didn't care about Ranger. Not yet. His time would come.

As Spike went to get past him, Hugh blocked his path. "This is what Ranger wants. You fight him now and they might kick you out. You're much more of a threat to him in the trials."

Although Hugh saw Spike's mouth moving, he lost track of his words; instead, he returned to the memory of beating Lance bloody. Felt the crunch of his face beneath his fists. His eyes battered to puckered slits.

"Hugh?"

A shake of his head and Hugh looked at his friend. "Huh?"

Spike paused for a moment. "Are you okay?"

"I'm fine. Why?" Heat flushed his cheeks.

The twist of Spike's features suggested he didn't agree with that opinion, but he didn't question it either.

Sarge then emerged from the dorm, his thick grey hair dishevelled from sleep. "What's going on out here?"

Ranger opened his mouth as if about to call them out. He then glanced at Hugh and Spike and shrugged. "Just warming up for training."

For a few seconds, Sarge said nothing, casting his eye over the three boys. When none of them added anything else, he said, "Don't think I'm not watching you three. *All* of you."

Sarge didn't have to worry about Hugh though; if this most recent encounter had shown Hugh anything, it was that he had the will to wait. He'd come to the trials with a plan. That plan was now only a matter of weeks away from being realised.

CHAPTER 34

"This is it, ladies and gentlemen." His voice amplified through the metal cone, Sarge paced up and down while addressing the crowd.

The bleachers had been packed for every trial, but as Spike took them in now, they appeared to be even busier, the spectators pressed shoulder to shoulder. They were stuffed in so tightly together, many of them wore twists of discomfort, and he saw several people throw displeased looks at their neighbours.

"With the five-point bonus for winning the final trial, we have three cadets going for first place and the right to be the next apprentice."

The ground muddier than it had been for any other task, the rain falling heavier over the past month as they said goodbye to winter, Spike stepped on the spot and felt the cloying tug on the soles of his boots. It wouldn't take much for him to lose his feet as he ran. In front of them stood what looked to be a maze made from the same wooden walls as the tunnels in the previous task, but the path didn't run straight this time. He hoped he wouldn't have to climb the walls again. He'd only managed to remove the last of the splinters from his hands and feet about a week ago.

"A maze," Sarge said as if confirming Spike's observations. "Simple really. The cadets have to get through the maze. And this time, Ranger, you can't run around."

Many of the crowd laughed. At any other time, the boy would have drank in the attention. With so much at stake, he acted like he barely heard them, rocking from side to side, his face fixed and his thick jaw tight as he held himself like he often did, assessing the entrance to the maze from beneath his heavy brow.

"You'll start in order of where you are on the leaderboard." A flick of his head to Hugh, Sarge indicated for him to stand at the front of the line. "You first."

Spike stepped in behind his friend and patted him on the back. "Good luck."

"We don't need it," Hugh said.

The Hugh from national service had died with Elizabeth. Not that Spike had stopped liking his friend, but he'd had to get to know a new person, and he'd given up trying to understand what went on inside his head most of the time. The boy behaved erratically and was prone to spells of introspective darkness. Maybe one day he'd open up.

Once Sarge had organised them in a line, Liz at the back, he said, "You'll start at thirty-second intervals. Like with the last one, this is dog eat dog. Everything's on the line for three of you. The only rule is you need to run the maze. Anything else goes."

A surge of adrenaline pulled Spike tense. He turned to look at Ranger behind him. The boy continued to rock from side to side as if trying to prevent his feet from being swallowed by the ground. He continued to stare from beneath his brow. He had it in him to kill for this. Hell, he already had.

Spike jumped at the sound of Sarge's horn and turned to watch Hugh run into the entrance, the crowd springing to their feet as they clapped and whooped. Unlike the tunnels, where many sections of the audience could see down them on account of them being straight, Hugh disappeared into the maze, and from the look of even those at the very top of the stands, no one could see where he went. Which also meant no one could see the underhanded tactics that one might employ to win this trial.

The next toot of his horn, Spike sprinted off, his feet squelching as he ran.

After he'd turned the first bend, the sound of the crowd grew quieter, muted because of the tall walls. What had been a public start now turned into a personal battle. He needed to get through it before Hugh to stand any chance of being the next apprentice. Whether his friend had a plan or not, Spike had his destiny in his own hands.

Spike turned right at the first junction, then a quick left. When he turned left again, a searing pain ran through the sole of his right foot, and he fell to his knees. Something was in his shoe. It felt like a nail. He'd tied his laces tight so they didn't get dragged off in the mud. For a moment, he held his right boot as if to remove it. Then he heard Sarge's horn. Ranger was coming.

Despite white-hot pain running through the base of his foot, Spike gritted his teeth, jumped up again, and took off. The pain he could bear. Losing to Ranger …? No way.

The sound of his ragged breaths as he managed the searing sensation while sprinting with everything he had, Spike watched the path in front of him. Left, right, left, straight ahead, left, right, right. Every step on his right foot hurt more than the previous one. Which one would be the one to throw him back down to the muddy ground? While he ran, the horn blew twice more.

His adrenaline running away with him, his thirsty gasps thrown back at him from the tall walls, Spike had no idea which way to turn next. Luck and determination would see him through.

Right, left, right, left. Then he saw it: an exit.

When Spike took another left, he emerged from the maze and looked around. He'd made it out first. He took in the crowd. The start of a smile lifted and he almost raised his hands aloft as he allowed his limp to get the better of him. It no longer mattered if the pain slowed him down. He could rest his foot now.

Then Spike saw Sarge appear from where he'd walked around the maze. He had the metal cone to his mouth. "You're the second through, William."

But Spike couldn't see anyone else. "*Second?*"

"Hugh's already been and gone."

It took that moment for Spike to see the weapons rack. A space where one of them had already been taken. A battle-axe remained among those left.

"Choose your weapon and get back through the maze," Sarge said.

As if on cue, Spike heard the shrill call of the diseased, accompanied by the loud roar from the crowd on the other side of the maze. If his foot hurt before, it now felt like his sole had been sliced open. What did they expect him to do? He couldn't run back through.

The noise level of the crowd rose, and Sarge's smile spread from behind his cone. "Surely you saw the twist coming?" He laughed. "The way back through isn't going to be anywhere near as easy."

CHAPTER 35

Spike chose the battle-axe, wrapping a tight grip around the thick handle with both hands before he charged back into the maze, squinting from now facing the low sun. The sound of the crowd behind him drove him forward like a fierce gale, his right foot alight with whatever speared it, his legs tired from five months of pushing himself to the edge. All the effort and still Hugh held the number one spot.

Upon re-entering the maze, the squelching grew louder because of the tight walls, which muted the crowd for him once more. When Spike rounded the first corner, he stopped dead. So did Ranger.

Just a few feet between them, Spike had a weapon and Ranger didn't. "What did you do to my boot, you cheating bastard?"

Blood ran from Ranger's nose, over his lips, and dripped from his chin. He grinned through the glistening crimson. "I found a nail. I took two from the muzzle I removed from the diseased. I figured they would come in handy at some point—a second chance to get you and your little friend if the first attempt failed."

The gloating somehow made the pain in Spike's foot worse, and he wrung his grip on the axe. He'd fantasised so many times about ending the boy, and now he had the chance to do it. The shriek of a horde closing in broke him from his dark thoughts. He had bigger things than Ranger to deal with. "I see you've run into Hugh. Or should I say, Hugh's run into you."

Ranger wiped his nose. "I got a few licks in. Reckon you'll be easier."

And there it was … A fight would only benefit Ranger. If Spike got dragged into it, he might lose. He'd definitely get slowed down. Hugh had already dealt with him. His hope of winning this rested on luck and determination, not petty squabbles with someone who shouldn't have the right to even call himself a competitor.

While yelling out, Spike charged. A clear confidence in the protector's son that Spike wouldn't use his weapon, he smiled, widened his stance, and raised his fists for the fight.

Then, instead of standing toe to toe with him, Spike leaped from the ground and led with his right foot. He used the sole of his boot to kick Ranger in the chest, driving the boy back and sending the nail even deeper into his foot. While roaring from the pain, Spike landed, left the protector's son on his back, and took off into the maze.

The sun had dazzled Spike on his way back in. If it continued to dazzle him, then he was heading in the right direction. The decision for every turn kept Spike facing the sun as he ran through the maze. Left, right, right, right, left, left …

The next turn revealed three diseased. Shoulder to shoulder, they blocked his path as they charged. Something about the wall of creatures in the enclosed Space nearly robbed Spike of his ability to act. Why the hell had he chosen a battle-axe? He had no room to swing it.

Nothing else for it, Spike lifted the weapon above his head and brought the large shining blade down on top of the first diseased. The other two jumped back as he split the thing's skull, a rush of warm blood spraying him. He kicked the now dead crea-ture into its friends, raising his axe again before ending them in quick succession.

After leaping the three corpses, Spike locked back onto the sun, jumping bodies of already fallen diseased clearly dealt with by Hugh before him.

The bodies vanished when Spike took another left, and a long corridor stretched out in front of him. Two more diseased appeared at the other end. Had he found a fresh path? A quicker one than Hugh?

Spike maintained his momentum, throwing another vertical swing at the beasts, taking down the first and then the second. It might have been unwieldy, but when it landed, the axe made easy work of the creatures. Maybe he'd chosen the correct weapon after all.

Now running with a limp as the pain in his foot got the better of him, Spike turned a right bend, the wind driven from him as he collided into someone. He lost his grip on his axe and landed on his back in the mud. The furious and shrill insanity of a diseased crashed on top of him. Its teeth snapped at him from the other side of its muzzle.

Despite the noise of the creature, the press of its body weight, its blood-red glare, and the same foetid vinegar reek that made Spike's stomach churn, he had the wherewithal to pick up the sound of more approaching beasts. If any more landed on him, he wouldn't get up again.

As the thunderous steps drew closer, Spike yelled, fought to drag his knees into his chest, pressed the soles of his boots against the diseased on top of him, and kicked it away.

The creature flew backwards through the air, and Spike jumped up, retrieving his axe. The diseased leaped up again, but he ended it with a skull-splitting blow. Two more behind it, he used their recently expired friend as a shield, holding them back while he turned their lights off one after the other.

The next left turn led Spike from the maze, the sun still dazzling him, the noise of the crowd damn near knocking him back in again.

The hands of a guard grabbed Spike and shoved him out of the way while another one sent more diseased into the maze.

His foot on fire, his ears ringing, his head spinning, Spike wiped the blood of the diseased from his face and looked around. He couldn't see Hugh. His heart beat faster. Had he won? The slain diseased were absent from Spike's path at the end. Hugh must have gone a different way. He'd beaten him!

Spike forgot his pain and bounced on the balls of his feet until his right foot gave out and he crumpled into the sludge. He'd done it. Matilda would get Artan back, and he'd won the five points he needed to be the next apprentice. Then he saw a broadsword stabbed into the ground. It was covered in blood from fighting in the maze: Hugh's weapon. But where was he?

The noise of the crowd rose again, urging Spike to look to his left. His short and stocky friend walked from around the side of the maze. The same guard who had dragged Spike out of the way so his colleague could send in more diseased grabbed Spike's shoulder. He didn't turn around, his world crumbling as he watched Hugh. He'd gotten out so far ahead of Spike he'd had time to wash himself clean and return.

"The water's around there," the guard said to Spike. "Go and clean yourself up for the ceremony."

The guard dragged Spike to his feet and encouraged him forwards with a gentle shove in his back. After just one step, Spike crashed down again, landing with a squelch as his knees slammed into the mud. With everything he'd been through over the past six months, he'd now lost it all to his best friend.

CHAPTER 36

Where Spike found the energy to keep going, he didn't know. The nail still in his right boot, it dug in with every step through the cloying mud. The same stabbing feeling over and over, it ran so deep his socks squelched from what he assumed to be his spilled blood. But he didn't care anymore. He just didn't care.

A guard led the cadets from the arena. Ranger, Fran, and Liz walked ahead of Spike and Hugh. Although Spike had his friend beside him, he didn't look at the boy.

Sarge waited for them outside, smiling as he clapped his hands. "Well done for putting on a good show. You all did well this year and were good value for the crowd."

That was all they were: entertainment for a baying audience. More kids sacrificed to keep the great illusion that is Edin alive. If enough people believed the bullshit, then it made it real. Why did they stick to their districts anyway? There were so many more citizens than guards or leaders. They could just say no.

Spike clenched his jaw against the burn in the sole of his right foot. The threat of tears stung his eyes, a lump had swollen in his throat, and his heart ached, but the pain helped ground him. It kept his head where it needed to be for the ceremony at least. There would be time to fall apart later.

When Spike finally returned to Sarge's motivational speech, the man said, "You all need to wait here while we get the podium set up, and then we're going to lead you in for the closing ceremony."

They were left alone for the first time that day. Spike still couldn't look at Hugh, but he glared at Ranger.

"What?" Ranger said, Fran beside him.

"Don't think you've gotten away with putting that nail in my shoe."

"What are you going to do about it? It's over now, don't you get that?"

Without a second thought, Spike rushed at Ranger. Hugh stepped between them and held him back. For a moment, Spike wanted to swing for his so-called friend. What did he want the apprenticeship for? What did he gain in taking it from him?

As if he could read Spike's thoughts, Hugh gave him his answer, turning to Ranger and saying, "I came here with a plan."

Ranger shrugged and raised an eyebrow. "Oh?"

"I wanted to prove to you that you were nothing. I wanted to show you how I could beat you on every task. How I was fitter, faster, and stronger than you."

A darkness clouded Ranger's face, and Spike noticed Fran gripping on to him tighter than before. "You didn't beat me on all of them though, did you?"

"Only because you took the coward's route on the fourth task."

"Some would say the smart route."

"A coward would say that."

Despite the reddening of his cheeks, Ranger managed to keep his tone level. "You've proven yourself. Well done." He looked past Hugh at Spike. "You've also beaten your best friend. And you know what? From what I've seen, you don't even want this apprenticeship, yet you're prepared to take it from him to prove a point to me. Some kind of pal you are. In fact, I wouldn't mind betting he's nowhere near as angry with me about the nail in his shoe as he is about you taking his chance at happiness away. His foot will heal while he's trapped in the agricultural district, making late night visits to meet with Matilda in the square."

Before Hugh could reply, the sound of Sarge's horn rang out. A guard appeared a moment later and motioned for the cadets to follow him. As Hugh passed, Spike looked at the muddy ground. From the way Hugh limped, he must have had a nail in his boot too. He deserved the pain and a whole lot more.

CHAPTER 37

Every step took more effort than the preceding one, as if the mud had grown a deeper thirst to cling onto Spike's boots. The nail reminded him of its presence every time he put his right foot down. He kept his focus on the ground and walked with a slow trudge. To look up would force him to see Hugh. At that moment, there was no one he wanted to see less.

A cursory glance showed Spike his dad, Matilda, and his mum were waiting in the arena with what looked like the other cadets' loved ones. No one waited for Ranger, but Magma stood amongst a line of protectors.

As Spike passed Matilda, his mum, and his dad, he kept his attention on the ground. He'd failed them. After everything he'd put them through, he'd failed to live up to his part of the bargain.

A podium had been erected to the right of the arena's entrance, pressed against the surrounding wall to give the best view to most of the crowd. The maze made it impossible for everyone to see. Made from wood and covered in fresh mud, the three steps of varying heights looked like they'd seen a lot of use. They'd once been painted white, much of the paint either chipped off or caked in old mud. The kind of thing they dug out twice a year and forgot about how filthy it was until the next time they needed it.

Hugh suddenly stopped in front of Spike, forcing him to look up. He stared at the back of the boy's head and balled his fists.

Spike jumped when Hugh turned around, catching him in his moment of fury.

"You deserve this," Hugh said.

"Are you winding me up?"

Hugh didn't answer. Instead, he charged at Ranger, screaming a shrill war cry before he tackled him to the ground. "Third," he shouted, punching Ranger in the face. "How does it feel to come third, you loser? You murdering piece of shit."

As much as Ranger tried to cover himself against Hugh's attack, the flurry of punches rained down on him in such quick succession, he didn't stand a chance.

Spike winced to watch Hugh smash Ranger's head from side to side. Blow after blow after blow. Spittle and snot shot from Hugh. "You piece of shit scumbag. Don't think this ends here, you murdering little weasel."

The crowd had fallen so quiet Spike heard the sound of squelching footsteps from Sarge and several guards rushing to Ranger's aid. Magma didn't, watching on with what looked to be disgust at his boy's inability to defend himself.

Over as quickly as it had started, Hugh twisted and squirmed against the guards' restraint as they dragged him from the arena. His heels left a trail through the sloppy ground. As he passed Spike, the fury left him. Tears streamed down his face and he said, "Well done, my friend."

His head spinning, Spike watched Hugh continue to fight while screaming, "Ranger Hopkins is a psycho! He killed Elizabeth and many others. He'll sell anyone out to get ahead. Don't trust the little rat."

Hugh fell quiet again when he passed Matilda. Spike strained to hear what they said to one another. Matilda looked washed out. Probably shocked from what she'd just witnessed. Although, after she talked to Hugh, the flash of rage he'd worn just seconds ago gave way to a similar pallid hue, his face falling slack. Whatever she had, it looked like it was catching.

After they'd dragged Hugh from sight, Spike let his body relax with a long exhale. He'd talk to Matilda after this to see what had happened. For now, he needed to focus on what Hugh had just done for him. By attacking Ranger, he'd just handed him the apprenticeship.

CHAPTER 38

Fran and Liz stood together on the platform closest to the muddy ground. It must have had a number three painted on it at some point, but Spike couldn't see where it had once been. Besides, the height of the step said everything it needed to. Ranger stepped onto the next one, the number two spot. He kept his focus on the ground, his clothes caked in damp mud, his ears and the sides of his head swollen and red. It took all Spike had not to offer the boy one of his own smug sneers, but he was better than that.

As Spike stepped up onto the winner's platform, the crowd cheered him. He smiled at them and tried to keep the pressure off his right foot to prevent his appearance of good humour being derailed by a hellish wince. After all these months, the thing he'd worked so hard for had finally happened. All thanks to Hugh.

Now he stood where he'd always dreamed of standing, Spike looked over at his family: his mum and dad with Matilda next to them. Matilda remained as pale as before, her cheeks glistening with her tears. Because she didn't have Artan with her, the boy must still be locked up. Now Spike would be returning as an apprentice, he could help get him free. Beside her, his mum sobbed and his dad wore the slightest hint of a smile. His boy had achieved something great today.

When Magma stepped from the line of protectors with a medal in his hand, Spike's heart skipped and his breath caught in his throat.

Dressed as if he was about to go out and slay the diseased, the thickset protector strode forward, Jezebel strapped to his back.

Every step the large man took towards him made Spike squirm. He and Magma hadn't exactly hit it off, and now he had to take an award from him that the protector might believe belonged to his son. A son who currently stood as a snivelling and bloody mess, publicly shamed and remaining there for all to see. What a pathetic weakling.

As Magma drew closer, two guards came with him and stood near Spike and Ranger. Maybe they were anticipating trouble. With Ranger's track record, they were right to.

The medal in one hand, Sarge's loud hailer in the other, Magma turned his back on the podium and addressed the crowd. "Ladies and gentlemen, boys and girls, thank you for making this trip today, for coming to witness the next apprentice. And we're so pleased to welcome them to the team. First, I'd like to say a few words about my boy."

The already quiet crowd fell silent. Spike looked at Ranger like everyone else. Even now, he had to have a moment to be the centre of attention.

"Ranger's mum died when he was just four years old. I did everything I could to be a good dad to him, but no matter what, a boy needs his mum, and I couldn't ever provide that."

Even beneath the mud and swelling, Spike saw Ranger's face flush. Part of him wanted to shout at Magma. To tell him it wasn't the time to be talking about Ranger, to not steal his thunder. But what did it matter? Let him have his moment. Spike had won.

He'd be the next apprentice no matter what Magma said about his boy.

"I wanted to say," Magma continued, "how proud I am of my son. Of the man he's become. Of the adversity he faces on a daily basis and how well he deals with it. It's hard to follow in a famous person's steps."

If Magma truly believed the words, he clearly didn't know his son very well. A toxic little shit, he did nothing but poison every social situation simply with his presence, but let him have his moment.

"You might want to know why I'm talking about Ranger and not William."

The crowd's attention turned from Ranger to Spike, and Spike shifted his weight from foot to foot as if he could work his way free of his discomfort.

"Something happened during training."

Dread sank through Spike's stomach. Where was this going?

"William and Hugh released a diseased from the pit."

"Ranger did that!" Spike said.

Magma ignored him. "And that diseased killed one of the cadets."

Spike felt Liz's glare burning into him.

"Jamie Swank died because a practical joke went wrong. Although, I think it's being generous to call it a practical joke, but we've held counsel on it, and I've been outvoted on that front. Personally, I think it was an all-out attack on my son."

The words exploded from Spike. "*Ranger* set the diseased loose."

"I think Spike knew he wouldn't stand a chance against him—"

"I *beat* him!"

"So he did everything he could to unsettle and destabilise him."

While his dad spoke, Ranger nodded along. The slump he'd stood with only seconds before lifted as he pulled his shoulders back and raised his chin.

"Because of that, we've decided that both Hugh *and* William are disqualified. So, ladies and gentlemen, boys and girls, please give it up for your next apprentice." His words caught and his eyes glazed when he looked at his son. "My boy, Ranger Hopkins."

"No!" Spike shouted, but the noise from the crowd drowned him out. Screaming so loud it drove stars across his vision, he stamped his right foot, the nail sending a lightning bolt of electric pain streaking up his leg. "How do you expect anyone to trust those in power in Edin when something like *this* happens? It's all a lie. It's all a big lie." The sound of the crowd grew louder and damn near drove Spike from the podium. No one heard his words, not even Ranger next to him. He looked at Fran and Liz on the number three platform. Fran nodded and clapped while Liz continued to glare the same accusatory rage she'd levelled at him since Jamie's death.

When the applause died down, Spike still standing the tallest of all the cadets on his number one platform, Sarge said, "You're allowed one final meeting with your loved ones in the gym."

Dazed and exhausted, Spike stepped from the podium, the nail in his right boot stabbing the sole of his foot again. He walked out of the arena to the sound of the crowd chanting Ranger's name.

As he passed his mum, dad, and Matilda, Spike looked up to see all three of them in tears, but something else sat in Matilda's grief. A moment's eye contact, she looked like she couldn't hold it in anymore. "They've evicted Artan."

It took Spike several more steps before the words hit him. Walking in a daze, tears blurring his vision, he barely managed his slow trudge from the arena.

CHAPTER 39

H ugh grabbed the withered arm that reached for him and jerked it hard to the left, the bone snapping where the bars halted its movement. Tears ran down his cheeks as he listened to another diseased pull away screaming. Where one left, several replaced it, so he grabbed another arm, the nails on its fingers scraping against his palm from where they'd continued to grow much like those of a corpse. This time he pulled the thing towards him until its face met the resistance of the cage it stood trapped behind. Spike had told him all about the hole. As long as he remained in the spotlight from above, the creatures didn't stand a chance of getting to him.

Since Elizabeth's death, Hugh had been constantly challenged to talk. Told that he needed to let it out. A hard yank to the side snapped the creature's arm much like the one before it, but he knew what he was doing.

A wail he had no control of exited Hugh's body, and he wiped his running nose with his sleeve. They said he needed to let it out, but he couldn't have let it out any sooner than now. Not if he wanted his plan to work.

His eyes burning with his grief, his broken voice echoed in the underground cell and the dungeon beyond. "You want me, you pieces of shit?" Hugh grabbed yet another arm and pushed it up this time, breaking it against a horizontal bar. Their weak limbs gave out like cornstalks when they met the strong metal. Every one of them retreated from where they clearly felt pain—although hard to tell how much—and no matter what state they were in, they remained ruled by their need to destroy.

He'd waited until now because now he could let it out. With Spike as the next apprentice, he'd given his friend the chance to be with his love, almost as if helping Spike and Matilda be together somehow filled the gaping hole left by Elizabeth's passing. Matilda needed Spike more than ever with Artan being evicted from the city.

The vinegar reek of the diseased mixed with the heady funk of damp earth. Hugh found it hard to see in the dark and through his blurred vision. How could they have even considered Ranger to be the next apprentice when a trip down here broke him? If nothing else, it had been his duty to help Spike become the next future protector for the good of Edin.

Before he grabbed another limb, Hugh heard his name and stopped. He blinked against his tears and the lack of light in the hole. The bright daylight shining down on him from above made it even harder to see into the inky void filled with diseased. The winter sun made the dark impenetrable by comparison. He must have imagined it. The diseased didn't speak.

Another pair of diseased arms reached for Hugh. He grabbed both of them, yanking them down with a deep *crack*!

"Hugh?"

"Wha ...?" Hugh spun on the spot several times, trying to locate the sound. He then smashed the heel of his palm against the side of his head. "Get out. Get out." Hadn't he been punished enough? Hadn't his mind tormented him too much already?

"Hugh?"

He stopped hitting himself.

"Hugh, what's happened to you, man?"

More limbs reached through the bars, touching Hugh's chest with their long nails as he stepped towards the sound. Without the glare shining down on top of him, the shadows gained definition. Amongst the twisted hatred of the diseased, he saw a face that took him a few seconds to recognise. It looked different from when he'd seen it last. Surely, he was imagining it? "Max? What are you doing down here?"

The Max Hugh had seen several months previously had more weight on his bones. Now he had sunken eyes and his clothes were too big for him. The boy shrugged. "This is my one chance to get out of the prison they keep me in in the labs."

"What are you talking about?"

"I'm an experiment to them, Hugh. You should know about that, you worked in the labs, right?"

"Because you haven't turned?"

"Yeah. They use my blood to test on. They sell me a speech every day about how I could be part of the solution. I could be Edin's saviour. But I can't go anywhere, and while my room is comfortable, a prison, no matter how you furnish it, is still a prison."

"So when will they let you out?"

"Never."

Hugh's mouth fell wide.

"I'm a *carrier*, Hugh. It would be too dangerous to have me in society."

Hugh's heart raced. Now he'd let the madness out, it didn't feel like it would stop. More hands reached for him, their long fingernails running down his front. "So you keep the hole stocked up with diseased?"

"Like I said, it gets me out of my prison."

"Wow. What's it like to walk amongst them?"

"They barely notice me. I've gotten used to it." Before Hugh could say anything else, Max added, "I heard how the trials went."

"Good news travels fast, eh? I've paid back some of the people who wronged Elizabeth, including Lance. I damn near beat the breath from his lungs before coming on the trials. The last piece of my plan was to humiliate Ranger by besting him in every trial and making sure he didn't get the next apprenticeship."

When Max didn't reply, Hugh shuffled forward to get a better look at him. Several pallid hands with surprising strength gripped his arms and shoulders. "What is it?"

"You haven't heard?"

"What?"

"Ranger's the next apprentice."

A shake took control of Hugh and he couldn't find his words.

"They said you and Spike released a diseased that killed Jamie."

Hugh balled his fists, and his entire body tensed. He then spun around, grabbed the closest outstretched arm, and pulled it towards him. While screaming so loudly it silenced the diseased, he shoved the creature away and pulled it, shoved it away and pulled it. Again and again, he dragged the thing into the metal bars between them, the creature's head clanging with every contact.

A deep tearing sound as the creature's arm finally came off in Hugh's grip, the beast yelled at a pitch so high it hurt Hugh's ears.

After discarding the diseased limb, Hugh fell into a cross-legged slump in the spotlight from the hole above and shook his head. "All that for nothing. With what's gone on over the past five months, they give it to Ranger anyway. I'm an *idiot* to believe Spike even had a chance. And an arsehole for making him believe it too. It was my one consolation to know he and Matilda would get the rest of their lives together, even with Artan gone."

"What?" Max said.

"Matilda told me they've evicted Artan."

"No, they haven't."

"Huh?"

"I've spoken to him. We had a problem with the prisons in the labs, so they moved us to the political district and put us in the justice department's cells. Part of me thinks they did it to show us how good we have it, but like I said, no matter how you furnish it—"

"We?" Hugh said, cutting him off. It had clearly been a while since Max had spoken to someone new.

"Me and the lady they brought in when we were on national service."

"Can anyone understand her yet?"

"No. But it turns out she's immune too."

"And what's it got to do with Artan?"

"I spoke to him. There's not a lot else to do in the tiny cells with nothing but a chamber pot in the corner. He happened to be in the cell on the left of mine. I was only in there for two days and nearly lost the plot, so I'm not surprised he was in the state he was in. It took me a full day to get his name from him and about half as long to work out he was Matilda's brother."

"When was this? Matilda told me he'd been evicted weeks ago."

"I only came back yesterday."

"So they lied to her?"

"It wouldn't be the first time. What I know for sure is that he was alive yesterday."

"They lied to her. I need to let her know."

"How?"

"There has to be a way. Max, you *have* to help me."

Silence.

"Max?"

"I don't know if they can punish me any more, so I will. Just do me a favour and hide this when you get out. I'd rather it didn't come back on me."

"What are you talking about?"

A piece of rope landed in front of Hugh. A second later, it was joined by a large wooden stick at least three inches thick and four feet long. "I use the rope and stick as part of my diseased herding tools. It's better than touching them, even if I am immune. You should be able to make a grappling hook of some sort with it and get out of here. Will you wait until it's dark so they don't know I've helped you?"

"Sure." While lifting the rope and gathering it up, Hugh said, "Thanks, Max. I won't forget this."

CHAPTER 40

Before Spike, Matilda, his dad, and his mum reached the gym —Matilda sobbing every step of the way, Spike and his parents staring at their destination without talking—Spike felt a heavy arm fall around his shoulders. Despite a violent urge to shake it off, he turned to see his old team leader.

Bleach leaned close to him and spoke just loud enough for the four of them to hear. "Hugh's in the hole, Liz wants to go home, and Fran will see Ranger whenever she likes, so I've spoken to the powers that be, and they've agreed to let you and Matilda spend the night together in the dorm you've been staying in. Just you and her for one night."

"So we can say our goodbyes? What, you want us to thank you for that?"

"It's the best I can get, William. I can lead your parents out of the training area and you can see them tomorrow?"

His foot still sore from the nail in his boot, Spike pressed down, the throb of it pulsing through him. What other choice did they have? He looked at his mum and dad. His mum was too lost in her tears to speak, so his dad said, "We can catch up in the morning, yeah?"

In the stark glare of his dad's strength, Spike wanted to crumble. He leaned closer to the man, stumbling into his embrace.

The deep baritone of his dad always took Spike back to being a little boy: a simple life when his dad was his hero and he didn't have to worry about a thing. "I'm so, so sorry," his dad said. "You deserved the apprenticeship."

"Ranger let the diseased out and pinned it on Hugh and me."

Although he aimed the statement at his dad, Bleach said, "No one doubts it."

It lit Spike's fuse, his words breaking as they burst from him. "Then why am *I* being punished?"

"Because it's *Ranger*. They're going to use anything they can to get him into the apprenticeship."

"It's bullshit."

"Welcome to Edin," Bleach said.

"I always thought …" Spike paused. "I always *hoped* that if I did the right thing and played by the rules, I'd be rewarded. I played the trials as straight as I could have. It makes a mockery of this entire city."

"While I agree with you," Bleach said while glancing at the other families heading towards the gym, "I'd advise against making a fuss here because I had to fight for you two to have tonight together. Go to the dorm and maybe don't say anything until you get there. This city's cruel. I'm sorry you're having to find that out so young, and while I respect your right to express it, I'd advise against risking what little they've given you."

After another embrace with his dad and then mum, Spike managed to thank Bleach. He couldn't blame his old leader for what had happened. On their way to the dorm, they passed the remaining families, who continued towards the gym. Spike glared at them and they stared back, the silent accusation of murderer emanating from every one of them. Ranger had remained in the arena, which was for the best. If Spike saw him now, they'd be leading him to a cell rather than letting him lead Matilda to his dorm.

By the time they got to the small hut, Spike had let the pain in the foot get the better of him, and he moved with a pronounced limp.

The second they stepped inside, Matilda fell into Spike's arms, and he held onto her shaking form. "They evicted him before Jan and I even had a chance to plead his case. They said he was too much of a liability."

What could Spike do other than hug her? What could he say? Just a few short minutes ago, he'd been standing on the podium in first place, waiting for the winner's medal and thinking how he could help his love rescue her brother. Now he'd lost everything, his consolation prize being one last night with the girl he'd intended to be with for the rest of his life.

It took a great effort to get the words out, the parting between Spike and his parents still raw in his heart, but this wasn't a time for balance, for having everything he wanted, for keeping everyone happy. He had to decide what he valued most. Several paths in front of him, he had to choose one. As hard as it would be, it seemed like there was only one correct choice. As he held onto his love, her body trembling with her grief, he whispered, "I think we should try our luck outside the city. I think we should wait for nightfall and leave this place."

Matilda stopped crying for a moment, pulling back and locking onto him with her watery gaze. She then fell back into him and squeezed harder than before, her tears rushing from her in convulsive bursts.

CHAPTER 41

In any other situation, Spike wouldn't have asked her to remain outside, but in her current state, Matilda needed to walk the path of least resistance. For once in their young lives, Spike probably had more to offer than her. After making sure she'd be okay, he snuck into what had once been team Minotaur's dorm. Who knew what names the teams had chosen now? Who cared?

Spike walked more easily on his right foot because Matilda had cleaned and bandaged it for him during the day. He still moved with a slight limp, but it didn't restrict him like it had. As he snuck inside the door, a leader he didn't recognise lay snoring in her bed. Like with all the other leaders, she kept her door wide open in what had proven in Spike's experience to be a useless attempt at catching cadets leaving when they shouldn't. The sounds of sleeping rookies issued from the darkness in the rooms on either side of her. Happy they were all asleep, he walked on tiptoes to the wall of broadswords.

Although much better than it had been, Spike still clenched his jaw against the sting in his right foot, held his breath, and pulled down two swords in their scabbards.

The snort of someone waking up snapped Spike rigid. He slowly turned to look at the team leader. A thickset woman with a tight afro, she sat up in her bed and squinted while staring at him in the dark corridor. Her voice bubbled from her throat. "River? Is that you?"

While trying to hide his limp and suppress his breathy response, Spike shifted closer to her door, but remained in the darkest shadows so she couldn't see him. "Yeah, it's me." He nearly put a voice on, but he didn't know what River sounded like —hopefully, River was a boy.

"What are you doing?"

"I have to do an extra shift on the gate tonight."

"I didn't hear about that."

"Sarge asked me to do it."

From the way the woman squinted into the darkness, Spike guessed her eyesight wasn't her strongest sense. Maybe that was why she trained cadets rather than became a protector herself. The silence lasted a few seconds, the woman squinting harder. "Come closer," she said.

His heart already on overdrive, Spike froze.

"Come on, I need to see you better."

"With all due respect, ma'am."

"Ma'am?"

"My mum raised me right. She said when you like a woman, you have to be respectful, especially when that woman is only wearing a nightie."

The squint eased on the team leader's face, her features falling until her jaw hung loose. "What are you saying to me, River?"

"I'm saying that I love you. I have from the moment I met you. And I know nothing can go on." He laughed. "I'm just a kid, right? But I also don't think it's appropriate for me to enter your bedroom." Heat flooded Spike's cheeks as he thought about the words he needed to say. His throat nearly locked up, but he kept going. "I already lust after you every day. I don't want to stoke those feelings by being closer to you while you're dressed as you are." A slightly darker patch of shadow to his right, he shifted into it so she found him even harder to see.

The woman stared, saying nothing for about thirty seconds. "Well, um … thank you for telling me. Um, I don't know what to say, but I think you're right. Now go and do your guard duty. Well done. I'll … um, see you in the morning."

"I'm looking forward to it, ma'am." Best not to push his luck, Spike did his best to hide his hobble as he left both the dorm and confounded team leader behind.

CHAPTER 42

"What kept you so long?" Matilda said as Spike helped her strap the broadsword to her back.

On any other occasion, Spike might have laughed about what had just happened. In the future, he might find it funny, but at that moment, he saw no humour in it and simply shook his head. "You don't want to know." He walked past her in the direction of the gates. "Let's get out of here while we still can."

The night limited their visibility, but as they drew closer, Spike made out the silhouette of the cadet on guard. "There's just one of them. That's good."

"Have you thought about how we're going to get out?"

"We have swords. They don't."

"Good point."

As they got closer, the cadet tensing at their approach, Spike recognised the tall and slim beanpole silhouette. "Trent?"

It took the boy a few more seconds before he said, "*Spike? What are you doing here? I thought you were on the trials.*"

"Look, Trent, Matilda and I are leaving the city tonight, so I need you to let us out."

It forced the kid back a step. "You want me to *open* the gates?"

"Yeah."

"Do you realise how much trouble I'll be in if I do that?"

"Have you seen we have swords?"

Before Trent could reply, Spike caught him on the chin with a right cross. It knocked him back into the gates, which shook from the impact, the chains at the top swinging out before slamming back against the wood. While holding his face with his left hand, Trent said, "What was that for?"

"You need to justify letting us out. Now you can tell them you were attacked." Spike drew his sword and pointed it at Trent. "Not only attacked but held at sword point. Say we threatened you and roughed you up, but we made sure we left you conscious to let us out and then lock the gates behind us. That way, the city's safe, and I'm sure they won't give a shit about us going missing."

Trent worked his jaw as if testing for breaks. He was just a kid, and Spike hated himself for saying it, but needs must. "I can cut you if you like? Make it look as authentic as possible?"

Even in the poor light, Spike saw the colour drain from Trent's face. Without a word, he walked over to the wheel on the right side of the gate while Spike and Matilda readied their swords in preparation for any diseased outside. As he turned it, the right gate slowly opened.

The gap no more than a foot wide, Spike led the way, his sword out in front of him as he peered into the darkness for signs of the diseased. When he saw none, he slipped outside, Matilda a step behind him.

The moon lit the space in front of them enough for Spike to see the change that had occurred since they'd been there last.

"They've nearly finished it," Matilda said as she appeared at his side.

The wall swept around in a wide arc, a gap where the new

gates would go several hundred metres away. Other than the space for an exit, the rest of the wall had been filled. The moonlight also showed the area was free of diseased, and they now had just one way in and one way out. It made their escape much simpler.

As Trent closed the national service area off behind them, Spike felt too guilty to thank him. They hadn't given him a choice. One last sweep of the open space confirmed what he'd first seen: there were no diseased in the enclosure. He noticed two large gates resting against the wall on either side of Edin's new exit. "It looks like they're close to finishing." He sighed. "It's a shame we'll never get to see it, especially as we gave so much during national service." After a moment or two longer, he reached across and took Matilda's warm hand. If he didn't say it now, he might never say it. "Come on, let's get out of here."

As they walked, Spike thought about his parents, and tears burned his eyes. He knew how much it would hurt them, but hoped they'd understand. After all, they liked Matilda and they'd want him to do whatever made him happy.

CHAPTER 43

A t least they'd reached the end of winter. The evenings were still cold, but if Hugh had been locked in the hole overnight a few months previously, he would have frozen where he sat, or at the very least spent the night in motion to keep his blood pumping. Sat in the spotlight from the strong moon in the clear sky, he kept looking up. No idea of the time, but it had been dark for hours. If anything, the sky had started to lighten a little with the first signs of morning. He'd waited long enough, but if he left it any longer, he'd miss his chance.

When Hugh stood up, it agitated the diseased around him and filled the space with fresh wafts of their vinegar tang. The funk thickened the air like the grease of a cooking animal in a humid kitchen. It clung to his skin.

After tying the rope around the middle of the thick stick, Hugh looked up at the moon again. In his left hand, he held the rope's slack, and in his right, he held the wooden stick like a spear. A silent countdown from three in his mind, he launched it up through the hole.

The stick went through on the first shot, but when Hugh

snapped it back down with a quick tug on the rope, it returned to him at twice the speed. He jumped aside at the last moment, the stick crashing into the ground where he'd stood as atrophied arms reached through the cage, pawing at him. Had he not had more important things on his mind, he would have fought back. Instead, he simply twisted free of their palsied grips and returned to the spotlight above.

A very slight adjustment to where he'd tied the rope, Hugh slid it a few inches one way along the stick and tried again, launching it up through the hole with a similar pace and accuracy to his first attempt.

This time, when Hugh tugged on the rope, its new position pulled the stick sideways. As he dragged it back down, it landed across the hole like a bar, the rope hanging down for him to climb.

After several tugs to test it, Hugh lifted his weight from the ground and swung in the tight space. It held. He then climbed out of there.

Just to breathe the fresher air aboveground sent a surge of energy through Hugh. He'd made it out; now he needed to get to Spike and Matilda … wherever they were.

Two wooden doors separated Hugh from the rest of the national service area: one that led from his cell, and the other the main exit. Both of them were bolted shut from the other side. Both of them broke like rotten wood when he kicked them. They clearly had too much confidence in the cadets not being able to get out of the holes.

Because his exit had been far from quiet, Hugh set off at a jog, finding the shadows and keeping a hold of the rope and stick Max had given him. He needed to get rid of them somewhere they wouldn't be discovered.

Even with the noise he'd made, from what Hugh could see as

he journeyed across the national service area, no one stirred. A sleepy atmosphere hung over the place, and it wore the low-lying mist like a cosy blanket. The dew-soaked grass squeaked beneath his steps, and he kept bursting through his own large clouds of condensation. He'd get to the gates leading back into Edin. If he got into the city, he could avoid capture long enough to get the message to Spike and Matilda in their respective districts. In a world with very little hope, he had to make sure they knew the truth.

So caught up in his thoughts, Hugh only heard it at the last moment: the sound of heavy steps from someone running close to him. One of the dorms was nearby, so he scooted around the back and hid in the shadows. While catching his breath, he peered around to see what looked like a cadet run into the dorm he'd chosen to use as cover.

Although he couldn't see him, Hugh moved closer to the dorm's entrance and listened to the conversation going on inside.

"And they attacked you?"

"Yeah. Two of them sprang at me and put a sword to my throat. They forced me to let them out."

"What did you do?"

"What they told me to do."

"Do you know who it was?"

"I'm from the agriculture district, so I know Spike Johnson. He had a girl with him."

Hugh smiled to himself.

"You're sure no diseased came in?"

"Positive."

"Okay. I suppose there's nothing we can do. I don't see any risk to us from what's happened, and you think they'll be long gone by now?"

"It was about an hour ago."

"Well, there's no point in waking anyone up. We're putting the new gates on tomorrow, so we all need our sleep. Go to bed and we'll tell Sarge in the morning."

Hugh waited for about five minutes after the boy had walked away, and because he heard no other sound in that time, he ran off into the night in the direction of the gates leading to the world outside. Whatever it took, he'd find them. At least he hadn't headed the wrong way, venturing deeper into Edin in what would have been a futile attempt to find his friends.

JUST THREATEN THEM LIKE SPIKE AND MATILDA HAD AND HE'D BE fine. That had to be the easiest and safest way out. Hugh saw the silhouette of one guard by the gates, but it took for him to get closer to see it was a girl. A small frame, mousy brown hair, and slightly sticking out ears. To look at her momentarily derailed him. She reminded him so much of—"Elizabeth?"

Images of her bleeding face. Of her turning into a diseased. A knife cutting into a stomach, tearing flesh. Ranger's face. Lance laughing. Hugh shook his head as if it would help him rid his mind of the chaos.

Just a few feet separating them, the girl said, "Uh … can I help you?"

Just punch her, threaten her, and get her to let him out, but the uncanny resemblance to his love paralysed him.

"Excuse me?" the girl said.

He couldn't do it. "I'm here to take over."

"But I've not been here long."

"I know. Sarge asked me to come down. They wanted someone with more experience. It's for your safety."

"What are you talking about?"

"Two cadets went outside the city earlier this evening. They attacked the person on guard. Sarge is worried more might try it and asked me to come down here and relieve you. It's not a night for rookies to be looking after the gate." It would be so much easier to threaten her.

"How do I know to believe you?"

"Go and ask Sarge if you like. What I know for sure is I have to be here and he'll kill me if I'm not." He saw Elizabeth's eyes turning red as the disease spread through her.

"I don't know."

Unable to hold onto himself, Hugh shouted, "Damn you, Elizabeth. Go and ask Sarge."

To see the girl wince at his outburst flooded him with white-hot shame. "I'm sorry, I didn't mean to scare you."

"Who's Elizabeth?"

Hugh shook his head as if it would get the images from his mind. "I'm sorry. Sarge intimidates me. If I don't do as he says, there'll be hell to pay, and we'll all be on the receiving end of it. Go and ask him now. I'll wait here."

As much as the girl looked like she wanted to say no, she watched Hugh with one eyebrow raised and stepped away from him. Her breathing had sped up, small clouds forming in front of her. "I'll be back," she said and ran off.

After he'd watched the girl out of sight, Hugh ran to the wheel on the left side of the gate and turned it enough to open a gap of a few feet. It would take her five minutes at the most to speak to Sarge and get back.

Only then did Hugh remember he still had the rope and stick in his hand. It must have added to the girl's confusion. And why did he call her Elizabeth? What an idiot.

Hugh peered outside. The way looked clear. As he lifted his gaze to the horizon, he saw the sky had grown lighter with the promise of daylight. It would certainly help his search for his friends.

Hugh slipped through the gap in the gates and broke into a jog. As he passed through the space where the new gates would be fitted and burst into the meadow, he discarded the rope. He kept the stick. The best weapon he had, he hoped it would be good enough.

CHAPTER 44

Maybe Spike imagined it, but as he lay in the pit with Matilda, the metal sheet covering them like it had the last time he'd slept there, he felt the itch of bugs crawling over his skin. Millipedes, centipedes, woodlice, spiders … he envisioned his body alive with the little bastards, a shudder turning through him as he thought about them trying to find a way into his ears.

Although Spike hadn't shared his paranoia with Matilda, she clearly couldn't sleep either. They'd spent the night talking. Maybe they could have continued on foot, but their odds of surviving in the ruined city in the dark were low. They were better off waiting for first light before making their move. They'd still have time to get away before the protectors reached the sprawling ruins.

Scared, sure, but Spike also felt free. Free from the arbitrary rules of an oppressive government. Free from the need to please people he had little respect for in the hope of gaining their approval. Free from the whims of powerful men who took their issues out on the city. What he'd give to stove in Robert Mack's head. The outside world had more to offer them than Edin. It would be a frantic beat, but they were now marching to the rhythm of their own song.

"Who'd have thought it?" Spike said. "All those times we spent lying on the factory roof as kids, planning an unrealistic future—"

"And now we're here in a hole, waiting to leave Edin for good."

"I'm so sorry that it's come to this. I wish we could have brought Artan with us."

A febrile response, Matilda said, "Me too."

The silence lasted for a few seconds before Spike broke it. "William."

Although he stared at the underside of the metal sheet, he heard the sound of movement beside him and felt Matilda look his way.

"When I went to see Bleach, his family called him Dave."

"I still can't get over that. I never had him pinned for a Dave."

"I think I've outgrown Spike. Spike is a name for someone destined to be a protector. The name of a naive kid who's willing to believe the propaganda and bullshit vomited from the mouths of men in power. They keep us like livestock, living in pens while we're sold a dream that few of us achieve. They maintain compliance by reminding us to be scared of the outside world. All the while, they live like kings. Protectors, politicians, and us. I would have never wanted it to be this way, and would do anything to reverse what's happened to Artan, but I'm glad to be rid of that cursed city. Will you call me William now, please?"

"Okay."

It clearly felt like a bigger deal to William than it did to Matilda. And why should she care? He'd only lost a name. She'd lost a brother.

The sound of thunder interrupted William's thoughts. He

looked up at the underside of the metal sheet as he released a long sigh. "Dammit. Not again."

"What?" Matilda's voice lifted a little. If she'd had the space, she would have probably sat up. "What is it?"

"Keep your voice down. We don't want—" The sound ran over the metal sheet above them again, and William said, "Too late. I *knew* we should have gone deeper into the city."

"You saw how dark it was last night. We pushed our luck just getting here."

"You're right. It's just, the last time this happened, the diseased above me didn't move, and it took three protectors to take down the horde who'd gathered with the thing."

"Spike?"

William gasped but said nothing. When he looked at Matilda, she appeared equally as paralysed by the voice above. They hadn't even made it to the next morning without being caught.

"Spike, it's Hugh. I'm on my own."

The way he spoke suggested William had a choice whether he revealed himself or not. The truth of it became apparent when Hugh slid the metal sheet away, daylight flooding into the dark pit.

His eyes on fire—blinded by the glare—William covered his face as he waited for his vision to return.

"I heard your voices," Hugh said. "What are you doing in there?"

Still blind, William sat up and heard Matilda do the same beside him. "Trying to stay alive."

"Well, it worked."

When William felt a strong grip wrap around his hand, he let Hugh pull him to his feet, standing on shaky legs as he continued searching for his bearings.

After a few seconds, William's sight returned. Matilda stood beside him, Hugh in front. "What are you doing here?"

Hugh shrugged. "I got out of the hole."

"They let you out?"

"No. I escaped. Max was down there."

"In the hole?"

"Moving diseased into it. He can walk among them now he's been bitten."

William's jaw fell loose.

Hugh had a stick in his right hand, which he held up. "He gave me a rope and this. I ditched the rope, but I figured I might need this."

As she retied her hair in a topknot, the hummingbird clip catching the morning light, Matilda said, "So why come out here?"

"I overheard a kid in the middle of the night say you forced him to let you out."

Both William and Matilda waited for more.

"Artan's alive!"

Too slow to catch her, William darted in Matilda's direction and clasped air as she slumped to the ground.

Her legs twisted beneath her, she looked up at Hugh. "What do you mean, he's alive?"

"Max spoke to him yesterday, in the justice department's building. Max and the lady no one could understand who came in while we were on national service are both immune to the disease. They're being kept in cells near the labs so they can run tests on them. They had to transfer them to the justice department's cells while they made some renovations to where they were being held. Max was in a cell next to Artan."

Tears shone in Matilda's eyes. "He's *alive*?"

"He's alive."

"Spik—uh, William, we *have* to go back."

Before William could answer, the shrill call of several diseased exploded from the city. The patter of clumsy steps followed. A second later, three creatures burst from the ruins. Blood-red eyes. Stretched maws. Flailing limbs.

By the time William had drawn his sword and Matilda had sprung to her feet, Hugh had cracked the skulls of two and used his blunt-ended stick as a spear, driving it through the eye socket of the third.

All three diseased down, Matilda said, "Wow. What have you done with the old Hugh?"

The look on his best friend's face turned William's blood cold. Hugh's tone was as stony as his expression. "He's dead."

Before either William or Matilda could speak, Hugh's attention had fallen on one of the three diseased. He walked over to it and bent down. It had a backpack strapped to it, which Hugh opened. He pulled out a folded sheet of paper. William and Matilda walked over and peered over Hugh's shoulder while he unfolded it.

"A map," William said. Highly detailed, it showed a long patch of land that pinched about two-thirds of the way up. In the northern part of it, it had what looked to be the ruined city, and then beyond it, a red line encircling what William could only assume was—

"Edin," Matilda said. "Do you think they were looking for Edin?"

"And what are all these other places?" Hugh said as he ran his finger over what looked like the locations of other communities.

As William stared at it, the realisation forced the air from his lungs. "We're not alone."

Hugh studied the map for a little longer, his thick finger running over the bottom third. "What do you think's here?"

What looked to be the depiction of a wall separated the bottom third from the rest of the map. Unlike the detail in the top two-thirds, beneath the wall was blank. William shook his head. "Whoever drew this map clearly didn't know."

The pause only lasted a few seconds, Matilda reaching across and touching William's arm. When he looked at her, her eyebrows pinched in the middle. "We *have* to go back to Edin."

What could he say? No? It didn't matter what they'd just found, they couldn't leave Artan.

"When we've freed Artan from his cell," Matilda said, "we'll leave for good. I promise."

"Let's not think too far ahead, yeah?" William said. "One step at a time; let's get Artan free first." As much as he tried to remain upbeat, a damp weight sank through him. If they went back to Edin, they had no chance of getting out again.

After she'd hugged him, Matilda then ran to Hugh and hugged him too. "Thank you for risking your life for us."

Hugh shrugged. "It's nothing."

William almost smiled. Regardless of what the boy had just said, the old Hugh remained somewhere in that broken form. With time, he'd return. As Matilda and Hugh walked back in the direction of Edin, William looked at the ruined city. When he'd been a cadet on national service, it represented the freedom of being a protector. When he'd approached it with Matilda, it represented the freedom of a new life. Now, as he turned his back on it, ready to face whatever punishment would come from the powers that be in Edin, it represented a closed door, a path trodden by a different William in a different life.

CHAPTER 45

O n their walk back into Edin—the morning gathering momentum, the fresh spring sun on their backs—William, Matilda, and Hugh hadn't said much. They'd dealt with several diseased on their journey home and remained on high alert for more, but it seemed like the day and the diseased were yet to fully awaken.

To walk through the gap where the new gates were due to be fitted, the gates themselves leaning against the wall on either side, tugged on William's momentum. What would it mean to give themselves over to the men in power? Then he looked at his love and got a lift from the hope in her eyes. He'd die for her. Nothing had gone to plan yet, and at least they still had a chance for something more when they freed Artan. Hope, no matter how small, had to be better than none.

William turned to Hugh. He'd lost too much already. "How are you holding up?"

The twist to Hugh's face suggested he might eject the same defensive response William had grown so accustomed to. *Stop probing my mind* or *talking's for pussies,* but instead, he sighed, dropped his head, and shrugged. "One step at a time, eh?"

A dejected response, but progress nonetheless, William moved closer to him and pulled him in for a one-armed hug. "One step at a time."

From the way the others stopped the second William did, they'd seen it too. About one hundred feet away from the gates, William kept his attention ahead. "Hugh, what did you say happened to the girl on the gate?"

"I sent her to talk to Sarge. I figured it would give me enough time to get away before they returned to lock the place up again."

"You figured wrong," Matilda said.

Only a small gap, but a gap nonetheless, one of the gates hung slightly open.

Before any of them could speak again, the gate shifted a little. Maybe disturbed by a breeze. Who was William kidding? It would have taken more than a breeze to move them.

A chill hit the top of William's head as if freezing water had been slowly poured over his crown. As he watched everything unfold, it ran down the sides of his face, locked a tight grip around his throat, and then dragged its fingers down his spine.

First, a pallid hand with long fingernails reached around the gate. A second later, a diseased stepped through the gap. Lank, greasy black hair, it appeared lost in its own world, grunting and snuffling as it emerged from the national service area. Clumsy with its movements, it rocked with a slight sway as if simply standing upright presented a challenge. Then it looked up. Red eyes fixed on them. Crimson streaks from where it had cried blood. Its brow furrowed. Its mouth spread wide. It then released a prolonged, rattling hiss.

END OF BOOK THREE.

Thank you for reading *Retribution - Book three of Beyond These Walls.*

∽

Support the Author

Dear reader, as an independent author I don't have the resources of a huge publisher. If you like my work and would like to see more from me in the future, there are two things you can do to help: leaving a review, and a word-of-mouth referral.

Releasing a book takes many hours and hundreds of dollars. I love to write, and would love to continue to do so. All I ask is that you leave an Amazon review. It shows other readers that you've enjoyed the book and will encourage them to give it a try too. The review can be just one sentence, or as long as you like.

∽

If you've enjoyed Protectors, you may also enjoy my other post-apocalyptic series - The Alpha Plague. Books 1-8 (the complete series) are available now.

The Alpha Plague - Available Now at www.michaelrobertson.co.uk

Or save money by picking up the entire series box set at
www.michaelrobertson.co.uk

ABOUT THE AUTHOR

Like most children born in the seventies, Michael grew up with Star Wars in his life. An obsessive watcher of the films, and an avid reader from an early age, he found himself taken over with stories whenever he let his mind wander.

Those stories had to come out.

He hopes you enjoy reading his books as much as he does writing them.

Michael loves to travel when he can. He has a young family, who are his world, and when he's not reading, he enjoys walking so he can dream up more stories.

Contact
www.michaelrobertson.co.uk
subscribers@michaelrobertson.co.uk

The Complete Alpha Plague Box Set

Protectors - Book one of Beyond These Walls

National Service - Book two of Beyond These Walls

Retribution - Book three of Beyond These Walls

Collapse - Book four of Beyond These Walls

Beyond These Walls - Books 1 - 3 Box Set

The Girl in the Woods - A Ghost's Story - Off-Kilter Tales - Book One.

Masked - A Psychological Horror

Crash - A Dark Post-Apocalyptic Tale

Crash II: Highrise Hell

Crash III: There's No Place Like Home

Crash IV: Run Free

Crash V: The Final Showdown

New Reality: Truth

New Reality 2: Justice

New Reality 3: Fear

Printed in Great Britain
by Amazon

87753918R00133